MIMI AND KY: THE BEGINNING

Yves Corbiere

CHAPTER 1

"Another, Miss Parks?"

Mimi had another. Henry had gone home around midnight, saying something about an early meeting, but she wasn't quite ready to leave. Plus, she liked being seen in a club alone; it added to her mystique. Only a confident woman goes out alone. Further down the bar two young women were looking at her with starstruck admiration. She imagined their conversation in her head: "That's Mimi Parks!" "No, is it?" "I love her show!" "Wow, I love LA!" Even though it was a common occurrence for her, Mimi loved being a tourist attraction.

The door opened. Mimi could see the barest hint of daylight sneaking its way onto the dark floor where glittering bodies still moved to the steady beat. It was the time of night when even the thump of the dance music was starting to feel dull and forced. She sighed and pulled out her phone to text Dennis to pick her up out front. During the season life was fast paced, hard work, and hard play. Now that the season was over, she felt a little lost. Tonight would end with no stories to tell.

She drained her glass, walked to the door and then out onto the street, strutting a little bit and maybe staggering a little too, but in a way she thought was probably charming. She felt all the eyes in the room on her back until the door closed behind her. The early morning was cool; dark enough that it still carried a hint of the immorality of the night, but light enough that she was looking forward to putting her famous self behind tinted windows. The sidewalk crunched uncomfortably under the soles of her pretty heels.

From the corner of a neighboring building, a pair of not-quite-human eyes watched her intently in the morning half-light. Mimi suddenly felt strange, off-balance. The sidewalk rose up toward her sideways; she would have screamed, but she couldn't find her voice. The world turned gray, static-y, electric.

For such a light figure, she hit the ground with a surprising thud.

The not-quite-human eyes opened wide and then turned surprisingly quickly into the eyes of a crow that flew to a nearby rooftop. From there he could get a good view of the street, the driver running to help Mimi, the ambulance, the lights, the end of the warm LA night.

Mimi awoke fully in the hospital. She thought she remembered an ambulance, and nausea; she felt woozy, confused. Things were clicking all around her, clicking, beeping, scraping. She heard wheels rolling loudly down the hall. A large monitor next to her head flashed green blips. Why was she in the hospital? She smelled hand sanitizer. It stung her nose. She looked around her bed. Her eyes came to focus on a nurse, giving her a dour look of judgment.

"What happened?" Mimi asked, and for a fleeting moment felt terrible guilt. She had been in trouble before: DUIs, a hospital visit after going overboard with drinking and painkillers. This was the same feeling, but different somehow. She was sore from head to toe. She could feel a bruise beginning on her leg. She tried to squeeze her hands tight, but her fingers hurt. The tape from her IV itched her arm. She scratched at it without thinking.

"You had a seizure." The nurse spoke but managed to maintain her purposeful frown.

Mimi recalled the club, the music, the women at the bar. "I wasn't doing anything. I just had a drink." Her head felt soft, achey. She closed her eyes but it hardly helped.

"We'll find out when your test results come back," said the nurse. Her voice was clipped, loud, backed up by a chorus of clicks and beeps.

Find out what? She didn't have the energy to think about it.

"We've called your father." The nurse attempted a comforting smile, but the effect was threatening.

Mimi felt teenage embarrassment fill her face. She loved her father and dreaded his disappointment. What had she been doing?

"I'm going to vomit," she said. It was a familiar phrase for her but the wrong context. Now that the preceding night was coming into focus, she couldn't remember drinking enough to be sick, although it wouldn't have been unusual for her.

The nurse gave her a deep tray to vomit into. She had been in a club, an ordinary nightclub. She even remembered being bored. She gave the tray back and looked at the nurse, who might have been saying something. The nurse clucked as Mimi's drug test results appeared in her chart on the computer screen. She was clean. Mimi's eyes went cloudy. She semiconsciously wiped a hand across her face. Then Mimi had the second seizure of her life.

Mr. Parks flew from Amsterdam to New York to Los Angeles. Dennis was waiting with a car at the airport to take him straight to the hospital. His timing was terrible; it was the middle of afternoon rush hour. Mr. Parks tried not to look out the window at the bumper-to-bumper cars, the hot, steaming, and sputtering LA traffic. He went over the phone call again in his mind. Fortunately, the call had come between meetings. Hearing that Mimi was in the hospital again, he had at first felt angry, but then the information he got was confusing. It wasn't another DUI; it might be drug related; it wasn't clear. He called the hospital from the car and was put on hold. The bright late afternoon sun glinted off the hood of the car. The hold music stopped abruptly. "Hello?" Mr. Parks said hopefully, but just as suddenly as it had stopped, the hold music circled back around to the beginning. He put his phone on speaker and set it on the seat next to him. Minutes on hold in traffic felt like hours. When a formal-sounding woman did answer, her voice was so robotic that he almost didn't respond. "St. Simon's Hospital. Hello. Hello. Hello…."

He dived for the phone, which had slid across the seat. "Yes! Yes, I'm here." She told him he couldn't talk to Mimi. Mimi was sleeping. She'd had another seizure. It wasn't drugs. If it wasn't drugs, then what was it? We're doing more tests, she assured him. Just as he hung up, Dennis pulled up to St. Simon's great glass façade.

"We're here, sir."

Mr. Parks launched out of the car, and nearly ran to the reception desk. St. Simon's prided itself on a non-hospital feel; the place seemed almost like a museum. Everything in the lobby was big and oak, nothing white. A cheerful young woman greeted him from behind a semicircular desk in the middle of the room. There were no sign-in sheets with contaminated pens and no name badges at St. Simon's. Mr. Parks was impressed. The receptionist took his name and said "welcome" as though he were at the Ritz and she had been expecting him. She sent him up to the second floor, where the place began to feel very much like a hospital. Maybe they only had the money to make the lobby friendly, he thought. He turned the wrong way out of the elevator, retraced his steps, and passed through some intimidating double doors with a radiation symbol on them. When he finally made it to Mimi's room, he peered through the long, narrow window in the wooden door. He saw Mimi lying there, her face gray, frightened. He had a sudden memory of her as a little girl, the first fever she'd had after her mother left, the way she looked at him with equal amounts of trust and doubt. Then, as now, he wanted to scoop her up and hold her. He opened the door and rushed to her side, but then stopped awkwardly by her bed. Could he hug her? She looked so fragile.

She looked up and tried to smile. "Dad."

"Hi honey, how are you feeling?"

"How do I look?"

He paused. "Like you had a tough night," he confessed. He sat down in a chair next to her bed.

"I feel terrible. They're sending me in for another MRI. They don't know what's wrong." She showed him the bruised inside of her elbow. "I must have had my blood drawn twenty times today."

"I'm sorry, honey. I'm sorry, I couldn't get here sooner."

"That's okay." She fidgeted with the IV tape. "You were in Amsterdam, right?"

"I got on the first possible flight."

"I would rather be in Amsterdam," she said wistfully.

"I don't think that's a good idea right now." He smiled. "But soon," he said hopefully. "When you're feeling better, we could go together." The words sounded strange to him. They both traveled constantly for work and pleasure, but never together.

Mimi laughed weakly. "I'm not sure you do any of the fun stuff in Amsterdam."

"Well," Mr. Parks equivocated, "I'm old. But I go to nice restaurants."

"Okay, nice restaurants. I'll give you that." There was an awkward pause between them.

"Oh, Mimi," he sighed. His voice wavered with emotion.

She bit her lip and then said firmly, "I want you to leave the room if I have another seizure. I don't remember them, but I've been looking up seizures on YouTube." She gestured to her phone. Its case was cracked. He imagined it hitting the ground as she fell, and the thought churned his stomach. "Seizures look crazy. I don't want you to see me like that."

"I can't believe they let you have YouTube in here."

"Oh, believe. This place is great."

"That's probably not good for your state of mind, being able to look things like that up on the internet."

"Better than not being able to."

"Mimi, you don't need to protect me. I've seen you through everything, remember? I'm your dad; I'm your best dad." That got a smile out of her. He continued, "I even saw you being born."

"That's not the same, everybody does that. Being born is super normal."

"I see you haven't lost your sense of humor."

She smiled. There were dark circles under her eyes. Her head was pressed against the pillow as though it were a heavy weight. She looked older, and too thin. He tried not to think about that.

"How are you feeling now?" he asked.

"Tired."

"What can I do for you, sweetheart?" He couldn't think of anything to offer. "Where's Martine?" Mr. Parks suddenly realized that Martine was at home and she probably didn't even know what had happened. "Do you want me to call her?"

"Yes," she said. "Please."

He left her room to make the phone call. Walking out into the brightly lit hall, he wished there were somewhere private he could go. He didn't want to talk about Mimi's condition in front of her, or anyone else, for that matter. He understood why she didn't want him to see her having a seizure. He paced as he waited for Martine to answer the phone. His shoes clicked on the polished floor, the shoes that he had put on yesterday morning in Amsterdam, where it was already tomorrow. He realized his feet hurt. He stood awkwardly in the hallway as nurses walked by with various items he didn't recognize on little wheeled carts. Then he heard Martine pick up the phone. She was in the kitchen; the water was running in the background. He felt as if he could hear the rooms in his house behind her, comfortable, secure, like a lifeline. It was the house in which he had raised Mimi. He spent most of his time now in an apartment in New York. The apartment was an easy jumping-off point for his business, but also he knew that now that Mimi was an adult, she would move out if he was there all the time. And he liked having her safe, at home, with Martine.

"Mr. Parks?" Martine said with her soft accent. "I thought you were in Amsterdam."

"I was." He paused for a moment. "But I just flew back. Mimi is in the hospital. She collapsed on the sidewalk. She had a seizure. Now she has had two." He couldn't think of a gentler way to say it.

"Oh, Dios mio!" Martine's voice was so loving, so concerned. It warmed him.

"They called me in Amsterdam. Thank goodness. I got on the next flight here. They should have called you. We'll have to get you onto her paperwork somehow."

"Of course," said Martine. "She's awake now? Is she talking?"

"Yes, she seems okay, just shaken." He whispered into the phone, "It's not drugs this time. It's…well, they don't know what it is." His voice returned to normal volume. "Can you come to St. Simon's? Room 204b."

"I'm on my way." She hung up.

Mr. Parks turned to go back into Mimi's room, but he saw through the window that she had fallen asleep. He stood awkwardly in the hallway, and then located a chair. He pulled it around to the wall across from her door so that he could see her face through the narrow window, sat down, and knit his fingers together. Communications of every kind were rolling in to his phone from the conference he was missing; it buzzed insistently from his belt, but he couldn't bring himself to respond. He wanted to give his daughter all of his attention, even if giving her his attention was just not answering the phone while she slept.

A woman wearing a suit and heels, rather than the ordinary hospital scrubs, came up to him. "Mr. Parks?" she asked.

"Yes."

"I'm the floor manager. I hope you and your daughter are both comfortable. We see a lot of celebrity patients. So, I just want to let you know that information about Mimi's condition and whereabouts will not be disclosed by any hospital staff unless it is for medical purposes. That's true for all of our patients; in fact, it's a legal requirement, as you probably know. But I know that you and Miss Parks are in particular need of privacy. You will find us to be nothing but professional here. Here at St. Simon's the security staff clears the parking lot of reporters, daily if necessary. No one is allowed to linger in their cars or watch the door."

"Thank you," he said. Mimi's fame was always a liability. Before she was famous, he thought he had it bad with just his successful company. But as soon as the first season of Mimi's travel show aired on TV, he had been on a steep learning curve about levels of fame. At any moment there was a price on her whereabouts. No wonder she drank so much! He was relieved that even in a hospital, she got some of the same special attention that she got everywhere else. It was comforting.

The floor manager stood there for a moment as though expecting more. Then she turned and walked away down the hall. He should have shaken her hand.

The last time he had been in a hospital, he was a young child with pneumonia. Hospitals back then had been big, greenish, tenement-like places. Nonetheless, his childhood stay there was a pleasant memory for him. He didn't remember the doctors or a floor manager. But he remembered the nurses. They were nice, clean; they spoke to him sweetly, spoiled him. The hospital had plenty of food, even ice cream. He had wanted to stay there. He cried when they sent him home.

He thought back to his young life, the narrative of poverty that played over and over again in his head. He remembered growing up with no refrigerator, no heat. He remembered trying to lure the cat into his bed at night to keep him warm, the time he ate ten hot dogs on a school field trip. The other kids laughed at him, but he didn't care. He was hungry. He remembered the first place he ever lived that had hot water. He was an adult by that time, living in a tiny apartment, but all he cared about was the hot shower. He was single then; no one wanted him. He had no money, no beautiful daughter, no LA mansion, no hundreds of employees. He thought about his first plane trip, Pittsburgh to Atlanta. That was right before he started SkyCut, his big idea. His life now was a dream; it never felt real. Sitting outside of Mimi's room, he tried to rustle up the feeling of that hot shower, how he had thought then that he didn't need anything else to be happy.

He kept his eyes trained on Mimi through the glass in the door, as though he was afraid she would disappear if he looked away. He studied her sleeping face. Her hands were clenched tight at her chest. He had not seen her that way for years, never as an adult. She looked so tired, small. She was small. She had gotten control of her eating disorder, but she stayed thin. She had to, for her work. He understood it, but he didn't like it. He wondered if her weight had something to do with the seizures. He cast around in his mind for a cause. There were so many possibilities, her eating disorder, her drinking, drugs, the stress of her fame, a bicycle accident she had had as a child.

It was hard to imagine the woman lying there was the same one he fought with just six months ago about her DUI. That was the fight that had ended in his hiring a driver. And thank goodness for the driver. Dennis had called 911. Dennis followed the ambulance, checked her in to the hospital. It was probably Dennis who picked up her phone, her purse. He wondered if Dennis had slept at all last night, if he was sleeping now. He didn't even know where Dennis was: in the parking garage, he supposed, if the hospital security hadn't kicked him out. He would give Dennis a bonus.

When he hired Dennis, his girlfriend at the time was angry about it. "Mimi is so spoiled that her punishment for a DUI is that she gets an employee!" Mr. Parks had no rebuttal. That girlfriend was on her way out anyway.

Martine, on the other hand, thought the driver was a great idea. When he asked her if she thought it was spoiling Mimi, Martine just said with her soft voice, "Everyone loves their children, Mr. Parks." Martine knew how to cut to the heart of the issue. He loved Mimi so much. The power of that love still stunned him after twenty-three years.

He loved her, but he didn't understand her. The world was different for Mimi than it was for him, not just because she was young. She was a native to wealth. She had made herself into a world-famous brand by pretending to be flirtatious and superficial on TV. At least, he liked to think she was pretending. He liked to think he knew her better than that; she had been a smart child. He had imagined a career for her as an astronaut, or maybe as a stage actress or taking over SkyCut. That, of course, was his real dream. But Mimi had wanted nothing to do with the business. It was a common complaint among his peers: *wealth has ruined my children*. But so far he didn't know anyone who was giving up their wealth to do anything about it. At least his kid was having success, albeit not the kind he had dreamed of for her. He alternated between being angry with her and proud of her, sometimes second to second. Lately, he had to admit, he had taken to ignoring her. It was easy to do, and now he felt guilty about it. He should have encouraged her more. He should have challenged her more. He wondered if anyone ever just had two seizures and that was the end of it. Could they walk out of the hospital tomorrow, no problem? Was that possible? What caused them? He could try to find a doctor. Would they know? Would they tell him if they did?

Martine swept through the double swinging doors with urgency but also gracefully, comfortably, as though she were stepping into her own house. Mr. Parks caught her eye and she smiled sympathetically as she walked toward him. She had made record time and was somehow also carrying a bag full of food. Her black hair was tied up loosely. Her clothes hung modestly on her middle-aged and slightly rounded figure. She was not a tall woman, but her presence filled the hallway so that the corridor seemed smaller with her standing in it. She was so much more real than other women. Martine had been his live-in housekeeper since Mimi was three years old. Mimi's mother had insisted on live-in help, and when she hired Martine she had said, "The best thing about this woman is that she will never leave." It was true. Martine had a daughter of her own, and it was clear that she was looking for a safe place to raise Paloma as much as she was looking for a job. But never wanting to leave was only one of the best things about Martine. He couldn't possibly count up all the things he loved about her; she taught the children to be kind and gentle, she was an adventurous cook, she was honest, and, unlike everyone else in LA, she was never on a diet.

He wished he could get a hug, but there was never any question that Martine would hug him. As far as he could remember, she never had. Now all of her attention was directed toward looking for Mimi.

"She's there," he said. "She's sleeping."

"Oh, Mr. Parks! There's our beautiful girl!" said Martine, and then she charged into Mimi's room without hesitation.

Mimi woke up. At the sight of Martine she started crying. Martine reached for her to give her a hug and seated herself on the hospital bed, pushing the tray table out of the way. She held Mimi's head and rocked her gently from side to side. Mimi was saying something Mr. Parks couldn't understand.

"I know, querida, se como te sientes," said Martine.

Mr. Parks waited, then fumbled with his words, "What else–what can I do for you, sweetheart?" he finally asked.

"Can you get somebody to talk to you? They're treating me like glass. I do want to know what's wrong with me."

"Of course, I will."

"If I'm going to die, I want to know it," she joked through her tears.

Martine made a cooing noise, "Do not say that, querida," she said, "nunca, never."

"We'll figure it out. And once we figure it out, we'll fix it," Mr. Parks said confidently.

He heard the words come out of his mouth, but he wasn't sure they were true. Mimi was a person, not a business proposition. Could he fix it for her? He walked quickly to the door, opened it, took a left out of Mimi's room and went to the nurses' station. A very young nurse was there. He asked if he could get some information about Mimi's condition.

"I just got here," said the nurse.

"Is there a doctor I could speak with?"

"Oh, no, not right now. I mean, unless you're having an emergency."

Was information an emergency? Mr. Parks wondered.

"Dr. Betts is in charge of her case," said the nurse. "You can speak with him tomorrow. He'll be here in the morning. He usually gets here around ten."

Mr. Parks was at a loss. Clearly there was nothing to do but wait; he suddenly felt as tired as he should have felt after an emergency flight back from Europe.

"Is there any way to get some coffee?" he asked.

The young nurse brightened up. "First-floor cafeteria. No one is in there, but the machine takes dollars."

"Thank you," he said.

On the first floor of the hospital, the night cleaning crew mopped in great, silent figure eights and a skeleton office crew typed quietly at computer terminals. The hall lights were dimmed, but the way to the cafeteria was well signed, which he appreciated. The giant room was silent this time of the evening except for the hum of refrigerators, a slightly malfunctioning fluorescent light, and the coffee machine. He got two cups. If Martine didn't want one, he thought, he could probably drink them both. He barely noticed, as he got into the elevator to go up to the second floor, that a tall, active-looking man wearing a faded baseball cap got in with him. The man kept his face turned away from Mr. Parks, but got off on the same floor and followed him out of the elevator and through the double doors. Mr. Parks' eyes were on Martine, who had left Mimi's room and was sitting in the chair he had pulled across the hallway. He didn't notice the man in the ball cap pause, glance into Mimi's room, and then keep walking.

Martine looked up as he approached and gasped.

"What?" Mr. Parks asked, concerned.

"Nada, I must have fallen asleep. It's just that, the man behind you looked, well, I shouldn't say that in here."

"Say what?" Mr. Parks asked.

"Like a ghost," she whispered. "Not a ghost," she corrected herself, frustrated. "There's no translation for it in English. *Nagual*, like a spirit, more than a man."

"Oh, I didn't think about him," said Mr. Parks. "But he wasn't a spirit, Martine. He was in the elevator." He handed her a coffee, which she took gladly. He added this to the list of things he loved about Martine; she drank black coffee at night.

"I guess spirits don't need the elevator." She laughed, but she sounded unconvinced.

"I think it's time to go home. You're exhausted," he said kindly.

"I don't want to go home."

"We'll come back tomorrow." He reached out tentatively and put his hand on Martine's warm hand. She squeezed back, strong, soft. He was flooded with gratitude for her. She loved his daughter. They were a team.

"I'll drive your car," he offered.

He texted Dennis that he would drive Martine back to the house. He didn't ask where Dennis was; he was too tired. Dennis sent him back a simple "ok."

Mr. Parks arrived at the hospital the next morning having slept a few hours, and was relieved to see a somewhat brighter-looking Mimi. He tracked down a doctor who explained to them that in many, even most cases, the cause of epilepsy was unexplained. So what does it mean, then? How can there be a well-known name for something without a *why?* Mimi realized that subconsciously she had thought that epilepsy was something you could have fixed if you had enough money and resources.

"Unexplained?" Mimi repeated. "But you know what happens, right? You know what a seizure is?"

"It's an electrical storm in the brain," said the doctor confidently. She was older than Mimi, but barely, probably a resident.

"From what?"

"That's the unexplained part. There are things that trigger seizures, some narcotics–" Mr. Parks looked uncomfortable, but the doctor continued without pausing, "–some infections. But there are seizures that, as far as we know, are untriggered."

"That doesn't seem possible," Mr. Parks said.

The doctor sighed and seemed to let down some of her professional guard. She gave them a friendly smile. "I know," she said. "I feel that way too. They must be caused by something, right? But we don't know what. The best we have right now are medications that control them, or sometimes surgery, but we'll try medication first. The brain, it's so amazing, so complicated. There's so much we still don't know about it. I wish we knew more. And we will, in the future, but I know that's not what you want to hear right now."

"Actually, it makes me feel better just that you sound like you're being honest," Mimi mused. "You know, when you're in the hospital it's hard not to be suspicious that everyone knows what's going on but you."

The doctor laughed. "We're trying to change that. St. Simon's wants to be on the cutting edge of this new friendly, helpful hospital movement. You know, we have plants everywhere and we pipe in natural light to the nurses' station through prisms in the ceiling. We don't want to be that creepy institution that everyone thinks about when they think 'hospital,' but it's hard. Some things change and some things don't. But we won't hide information from you guys if we can help it. Or, okay, I won't hide information from you if I have it."

"You're a resident, right?" asked Mr. Parks.

"Yes."

"Is it too personal, or can I ask you if they're working you to death?"

Mimi cut in to explain. "My sister is a fourth-year medical student. He's worried about her." She always referred to Paloma as her sister. It was simpler that way.

The young doctor laughed. "St. Simon's is working on that too," she said. "But all change is slow in medicine."

"Change is slow in most businesses," said Mr. Parks sympathetically. "Well, try to take care of yourself. We need people like you to last."

A thought occurred to Mimi. "Are you going to stay in LA? When you have your own practice, can I be your patient?" she asked.

"Oh, wow, I would be honored! Oh, but that makes me feel sad." The young doctor frowned.

"Why?"

"It's my last day on this floor and I know they'll try to keep you for at least a little longer, and I *do* want to be your doctor."

Mimi felt a wave of crushing disappointment that she realized was foolish. She had known this woman for about ten minutes and yet she was sorry to hear her say she wouldn't be coming back. It was her second day in the hospital and she was losing the only ally she had found.

"What's your name?" Mimi asked.

"Cora Hutch-, Cora Mancuso. Wow, sorry, brain slip. I just…I just got married." She blushed bright red.

"Congratulations!" said Mr. Parks.

"Thanks. It's just odd because I have practiced saying 'Dr. Hutchins' in the mirror since I was eight years old. And now I'm Dr. Mancuso. They haven't changed my badge yet." She frowned at it. "They'll probably never change my email."

That afternoon, Mimi had another seizure, a long one. A different doctor came to see her, and she was disappointed. She was hoping to see Dr. Mancuso one more time. The new doctor looked concerned, but provided nothing that Mimi considered information. Numbness ran down Mimi's legs. It was terrifying at first. She thought she would lose feeling entirely. It was like pins and needles, but infinitely worse. She rubbed them and they hurt, they shook. She limped to the bathroom. And she was sore, so sore, although that was supposedly normal. She couldn't believe that two days before she'd been lifting weights with her personal trainer trying to improve her deltoids for a photo shoot for a perfume ad.

Days passed. Time felt nebulous to Mimi at the hospital. Her father and Martine came and went, brought her bags of comforting foods, putting particular treasures on Mimi's nightstand so that it filled up with favorite cinnamon rolls, olives stuffed with blue cheese, cayenne popcorn balls. Mimi made a show of being happy to see these things when Martine put them down, although she had little appetite. She offered them to the nurses and found out that Martine had been cooking for them too.

Mimi's phone buzzed and rang and buzzed but she couldn't bring herself to answer it.

They ran test after test for a week but every test came back negative, inconclusive, or just confusing. They tried different combinations of medications, but it was the same for her day after day: one or two seizures, soreness, exhaustion. She became despondent. They made an appointment for her to see the hospital counselor.

The next day a spare woman with impeccably styled blonde hair came in and sat at the foot of her bed.

"You like to be called Mimi?" the woman asked.

Mimi gave her a quizzical look, and thought—but didn't say—that since she was on the cover of last month's *Celebrity* magazine as "Mimi," that was probably a safe assumption.

The woman continued as if she didn't notice Mimi's stare. "Sudden illness can be very disorienting."

"That makes sense," said Mimi. What could she say to this woman who had never had a seizure?

"I'm here if you want to talk," said the spare woman. She had thin lips and her glittery lipstick had separated from her lip liner.

The silence between them was awkward. Mimi was accustomed to forestalling such moments and, even though she thought she shouldn't have to, she tried to make the woman more comfortable. "I just feel really lucky that my dad is so supportive. I know I can count on him no matter what." It was what she would have said in a television-style interview. The words came easily to her, no thinking.

"Yes, what a great father. I notice that you haven't called your mother."

She wanted to slap the woman. "No," she said politely. "We're not close."

There was an awkward silence again, but Mimi didn't feel that she wanted to repair this one. Thoughts of her mother always gave her a headache, and this moment was no exception, but she didn't want the woman to see her flinch. Mimi had a great relationship with her father, and here her father was supporting her. Why wasn't that enough? Because when you're rich and famous, everyone wants your pain. Your pain is like cake to them, she thought. They want to see you cry about your mother. Fat chance, skinny counselor lady.

The spare woman was speaking again.

"Is it hard for you that you don't have a firm diagnosis? I have heard from other patients that each new test can feel like you're facing down that new possible future, like being diagnosed with many frightening illnesses one after another."

That, at least, was true. Every time Mimi got another blood test or MRI or EEG it seemed like they were actively looking for a worse possible life for her. With some of the more debilitating degenerative diseases that she had been tested for, she had wondered if she even wanted to know the results. But so far nothing came back really positive. Was that worse or better? Mimi felt like asking the counselor if she'd ever been sick. Have you ever been sore for no reason that you remember? Have you ever had to be escorted limping to the bathroom? Woken up on the floor with a mouth full of blood, covered in bruises that your own stupid body managed to create? Have you ever peed yourself? Regained consciousness surrounded by strangers and covered in vomit? They should hire someone with experience, she thought, not a degree, real experience. But then, she supposed that every disease would need its own counselor.

"That's probably the most frustrating thing," said Mimi coolly. She noticed out of the corner of her eye that something was moving on the windowsill. She turned to see the flapping of wings as a large crow made its way slowly to land and look in her window.

The counselor looked out the window startled. "My my, that's a big crow! Or is it a raven when it's that big?"

"It's a crow," said Mimi. "Look at the square tail. Ravens have wedge-shaped tails." She wouldn't have known that except that it had come up in the London episode of her show. She was flirting with a guide at the tower of London, and he taught her how to tell a raven from a crow. It's not just size. There are some very large crows in the world. London had made a good show. Their connections there had British humor, but not too much, and the Tower of London is fascinating to Americans. It's fun for them to imagine their treasonous ancestors locked up there, mocked by ravens, living off rats.

Mimi supposed she was lucky she hadn't collapsed mid-season, fallen off a parapet while being filmed for an episode on Welsh cheeses and castles. She didn't know if she'd be able to do another season, and it made her grimace to think about it, all the commitments she wouldn't be able to make unless she was somehow better by next week, which was looking less and less likely. Mimi met the crow's eyes. It stared back at her steadily, confidently.

"I know that illness can be very depressing," the counselor was saying. "I'm not a doctor, but if you feel as though you need help with that aspect of your illness, let me know and I'll recommend that the psychiatrist come see you."

Mimi was transfixed by the crow. Gazing eye to eye, it was as though he was peering at her thoughts.

"Mimi?"

"What?" She tore her gaze away from the window and looked at the counselor.

"Do you want to see a psychiatrist?" the counselor said pointedly.

"Thanks," said Mimi. "I probably don't need that right now." She felt like the last thing she needed was more medication. She looked back at the crow. It was still staring at her, its eyes both glassy and depthless. Mimi wished she could turn into a crow and fly away too. She was so lost in the bird's eyes that she barely noticed the counselor leaving. The door slammed, shaking Mimi out of her gaze. She looked at the door, but when she looked back to the windowsill, the crow was gone. Mimi got a sudden chill and pulled the sheet up around her shoulders. She had a fleeting feeling that she had been tested, that she had given too much away, even though she had hardly said anything at all.

When a nurse came in later, Mimi said, "I don't want to see the counselor again unless it's like, you know, required."

The nurse laughed. "It's not required."

CHAPTER 2

It was all over the internet.

#EricEllsworthForPresident

Without thinking, Eric gave a joyous leap and threw his phone high in the air. He knew he would catch it. As it came down, he swiped it with one hand. But he would have to be more careful, he thought; people can't think you're reckless when you're running for president. He looked around and breathed a sigh of relief. No one had seen him except a solitary crow perched on a streetlight. Who throws a seven-hundred-dollar phone? The person who is a hundred percent sure, that's who.

It was a warm, end-of-summer day in Washington, DC, and Eric Ellsworth felt like he was twenty-five again. Henry had told him the effects would take some getting used to, an adjustment period, but he could hardly think why. He felt like he was flying. #EricEllsworthForPresident wasn't the only thing going well in his life. He'd made some investments in a military contracting company, Sonintech, that were paying off surprisingly well. Apparently they had some big breakthrough in technology? Biochem? It wasn't clear. It was a quiet company, not much marketing but steady earnings in military contracts. That he could invest in the company privately despite being on the Armed Services Committee was a wonderfully lucrative loophole. Even though he'd been a senator for six years, it still amazed him that some things were not illegal. Despite exposé after exposé, no strict legislation challenged the lawmakers' ability to invest privately, even in companies directly affected by the legislation they were writing. This country was too in love with wealth to put an end to real insider trading, and Eric was thankful for that. If they wanted a presidential candidate who wasn't investing in the same markets he or she influenced, they would have to look on another planet. Certainly, none of his known opponents would question him on his private investments. They wouldn't want to be questioned on theirs.

But would any of them question what Henry had offered him? That was more complicated. Of course, it would never come to light; how could it? It was not something even the tabloids would be willing to cover. Eric lived such a normal life; it would seem insane to accuse him of dabbling in the occult. And he was sure that Henry had an effective way of staying out of the papers. Actually, now that he thought about it, it had been Henry who had recommended Sonintech. The owner was Henry's friend, a friend Eric had never met. He had only met a few of Henry's friends, but every one of them could be instrumental in his election. He was flattered to be counted among them. He tried to put out of his head the question of *why* he was counted among them.

He strode through the parking garage and clicked open the door of his little black sedan. It was a one-meeting day. He'd scheduled a light day because he'd thought he'd be tired from the trip, but nothing could be further from the truth. The way he felt now, he had enough energy to get through a hundred meetings. Still, he wasn't sorry to have the afternoon off. As he pulled out onto Interstate 66, he was humming a little tune to himself. He realized, with some embarrassment, that it was "Hail to the Chief," and he tried to nonchalantly change it to "God Bless America" even though no one was listening. He headed west toward his house in Sterling. The flat, lush, green, semi-swampland of DC transitioned to the low rolling hills of Northern Virginia. He noticed that he was running out of gas. He felt so good, it almost surprised him, but then a voice in his head said, *Really? You expected Henry to fill up your tank with gas from across the country?* And yet Eric couldn't quite shake the feeling that if Henry wanted to, Henry could.

When Eric had gotten that first phone call from Henry, he could hardly believe it. There on the other end of the line was a calm, serious voice telling Eric that he could help him run for the presidency. Eric thought that was twenty years away. He would have hung up the phone except for that strange forewarning. He had been in the elevator with Senator Kelsey, a senior leader whose clout you had to appreciate, even if you didn't admire his bullish personality. They had only spoken a few times outside of the regular Washington small talk. Kelsey got into the "members only" elevator and said to him, "Good, I was looking for you, Ellsworth. Whatever you do, take my next phone call." The elevator dinged the next floor and Kelsey strode out as soon as the doors opened, without looking at Eric. Eric had been too surprised to respond. That afternoon, the call from Henry was a transfer from Kelsey's office. Still, Eric almost didn't meet with Henry. It just seemed too improbable. How could someone have that kind of wealth and power and yet Eric had never heard of him? Eric had been a fool to doubt. The second he had taken Henry up on the offer of a quiet drink, his approval ratings began to rise. He had gotten little pieces of national attention. Then there was that article about him in *Forbes*. He could see the cover clearly in his mind—"Can This Guy Save Congress?"— with a picture of him, Eric, smiling. No doubt about it; he looked good on the cover of a magazine.

He felt, yes, like he was flying. That was the only way to describe it. He couldn't imagine anything going wrong today, on a day after he'd met with Henry. This was only their second meeting, but hadn't the first one yielded the cover of *Forbes*? And yet he had a nagging suspicion. Maybe it was his Puritan roots. He hadn't done anything wrong. Anyone is allowed to have a drink with a wealthy benefactor. But there was surprisingly little about Henry anywhere on the internet. He hadn't questioned Kelsey; he didn't want to seem ungrateful. But if Henry was in fact someone he didn't want to be associated with?

No one would know he had been there. And maybe that knowledge itself was the source of the nagging guilt. He couldn't quite shake the feeling that he was being watched or followed. He kept looking over his shoulder for the telltale signs of reporters. Nothing. He stopped at a gas station, filled the tank, and went in to buy a bottle of water. His eyes were irresistibly drawn to the scratch lottery cards. He had never felt so lucky. He bought two.

"Senator?" said a low voice.

Eric jumped. He hadn't even realized there was a man behind him in line. The man was tall, athletic, wearing a faded baseball cap.

The gas station owner looked at the two men from his perch behind the counter. He recognized the senator. The other man, he thought, looked suspicious. It was almost as though the senator was clear and the other man was blurry. He blinked at them, but the effect was the same. He glanced up at the security cameras, as though they could somehow tell him about the stranger. The senator didn't seem to notice anything amiss.

"Yes, what can I do for you?" Eric turned around with his campaign-winning smile.

"You look lucky today, sir," said the man in the cap, gesturing to the cards. "I hope you win."

Eric couldn't resist the opportunity to gain a vote. He handed the man one of his scratch cards. "Let's hope we're both lucky today. " He smiled.

The man took the card but returned no expression. If anything, it looked as if he was searching Eric's face, maybe even smelling him? His head moved slightly side to side, eyes half closed under the brim of his cap. But Eric was too cheerful to let one strange interaction affect his mood. There were a lot of peculiar people around Washington. Eric walked back to his car whistling. He didn't notice that the man barely looked at the card. Eric scratched his own. It was a ten-dollar winner. He paused, but decided he would redeem it next time. He got into his car and pulled away. The man in the baseball cap held his nose up to the wind appreciatively, and then disappeared behind the gas station. The station owner watched him out the window, looked at the parking lot. He realized the man in the baseball cap had no car. This was a highway station. The gas station owner grabbed his handgun from the drawer, tucked it in his pocket, and walked behind the building. He didn't like the look of that guy. What look? He couldn't remember a single distinguishing characteristic except the faded cap. The senator, on the other hand, looked like a man you would vote for. The station owner rounded the corner of his building and stopped, surprised. No one was there. All he could see was a large crow flying away. Just to be sure, he cautiously approached the dumpster, gun drawn beneath his jacket. There was the card, still unscratched. He picked it up and brought it back inside. It was not a winner.

Sarah Ellsworth stood in her living room, her feet rooted to the ground, her chest heaving. Her breath was coming in short bursts as though her anger had depleted the oxygen in the room. She stared at the fresh vacuum lines in the carpet. Fresh vacuum lines in a beige carpet, what a ridiculous life! But she couldn't see a way out. She had reached the point where even in her own head she called herself "The Senator's Wife."

She had made herself perfect, even perfect at being imperfect. Last year she admitted with casual intimacy to a large crowd at a campaign fundraiser that she struggled with browning the thanksgiving turkey, giving them a wink. When she married Eric she had believed in him, or at least *agreed* with him, but now? Could she stand next to him, knowing what he had done, for the next four years? Eight years? Forever? Because it would feel like forever. Or could she mire him in a messy divorce just as he was on the verge of every man's dream? Was it a man's dream? Perhaps it was the dream of a child. And he was like a child, thinking only of his own desires. She wasn't sure she wanted him to be her president. But she had married him. She turned the receipt over again in her hand, for the hundredth time.

He had been in LA.

She retraced their conversation. He said he was going to meet with some possible big contributors to his campaign, his upcoming campaign, in Ohio. If those contributors were really in LA, why not tell her he was going to LA? Because he was meeting *her,* of course. He was meeting the woman that he had confessed to having an affair with a year ago. He had met her in LA, at a fundraising event. He had an affair for six months and then told Sarah about it on her birthday in a poorly timed attack of guilty repentance. He stopped the affair, or so he said. At least he had chosen someone with some sense of propriety. There had been no leak, no public embarrassment. Sarah knew she could say nothing. Wasn't she also dependent on his career? Apparently, the other woman had similar constraints, a movie star? Sarah had never asked. It made her blood pressure rise just thinking about it.

Their house was quiet, their perfect, stupid, stinking house. Afternoon light poured in the windows; birds chirped. A large and rather precocious crow was stalking the bird feeder, hanging on one side of it, then the other. The feeder swung wildly under the large bird's weight, and the other birds flew around, agitated. She hated Eric Ellsworth. Why had she taken his rotten, cheating name? She thought the crow at the feeder was looking at her a little too intently. Stay sane, she thought.

She heard Eric's car drive into the driveway and sucked in a deep breath. His footsteps were light. He was whistling. He sounded happy. She heard him hang up his coat, put down his keys.

She stayed where she was in the living room, transfixed in the moment before their inevitable fight. He was magnificent, she thought, especially since he had returned from his trip. There was something about him. He was glowing, magnanimous. They had made love last night when he returned. How could he, when he'd been in LA with another woman? How could he even look at her, much less touch her? She thought she could tear out his heart with her fingernails, or maybe her own heart. Would he regret it if he found her lying on that clean, vacuum-striped carpet with her heart in her hand? Would he just cover up her suicide, or play the sympathy card and use the tragedy in his election? Would he pretend it wasn't his lying, cheating ways that drove her to it? Was there ever a man in the world who hadn't had an affair? They run statistics on these kinds of things. But the statistics can't be right. She would lie about it to anyone.

He rounded the corner of the living room and stopped when he saw her there, breathing, staring at him.

"Sarah?" he said tentatively.

"I don't go through your pockets," she started, almost whispering, her breath was so labored. "I don't look at your phone."

"What are you talking about?"

There was a moment of silence between them and then she blurted out, "You didn't come back from Ohio yesterday!"

"Oh, no." He looked terribly guilty.

"No! No you weren't in Ohio! What were you doing in LA? You bought–" she looked at the receipt even though she had memorized it. "You bought a water bottle in LA yesterday."

"Honey, you think I–? It's not what you think!"

"What do I think?"

"I assume you think that I was…" here he paused, struggling to get the words out. "…with, with another, with a woman. But I assure you I was not. She doesn't… she doesn't live there anymore anyway." He hurried past that thought as her eyes started to smolder. "I was meeting a donor. It's just, I said Ohio because this donor doesn't want to be associated with me yet. *He* is a very private person."

"So private that you had to lie to me?"

"Sarah, I'm sorry. I lied to everyone; it was just easier to lie to you too in case you talked to someone about where I was. I shouldn't have. I just did to make it easier. This is big money. This is really, really big money. And this is not a guy who wants everyone in the world to know his business."

"Oh? What kind of business is that?"

"Sarah."

"Secret business?"

"Please, honey," he pleaded.

"Right, it sounds like this *guy* is a pillar of society."

"Sarah, don't make assumptions."

"So you're not having an affair again, you're just taking donations now from Al Capone?"

He gave her a look that said she almost wasn't wrong. "Not, not like that." He knit his eyebrows. What idiot keeps a cash receipt? he thought.

"Who is this donor?"

He took a deep breath. "I'd rather not tell you."

"Then I will walk right out that door." Sarah gestured to the foyer. She felt his panic, and she liked it. "Need I remind you how a pending divorce would affect your candidacy?"

"What kind of threat is that?" He tried to sound calm, but the pitch of his voice started to rise.

"The kind you will listen to! The kind that threatens the only thing that's important to you anymore."

"Sarah, that's not fair. You are important to me." He was not lying, but partly, yes, their marriage was important to him because it was important to his career. "I have made mistakes. But I have been honest with you about them. Yesterday, I was meeting a donor."

"Eric, you need to give me a reason to believe you, pronto, and that better start with the name of this gangster who's funding your campaign."

There was a moment of silence. Even the birds outside seemed still.

Eric thought about lying, making up a name, but if she found out...she was right. She could ruin everything. She might be the one person in the world who could most easily ruin everything. Yet Henry had been cagey, so secretive about their relationship. Eric didn't really know what he did, where the money came from. He weighed them against each other in his mind. But Sarah was right. She could ruin him. Finally, Eric sighed and said, "Henry. Henry Halstead."

He couldn't tell from her look whether she believed him or not.

"Sarah please don't...." He was about to say, *don't look him up*, but realized how that would sound to her.

"Don't what?"

"Believe me, please. At least believe me when I'm telling the truth."

The set of her jaw could have brought on an ice age. She left the room.

As soon as he was alone, Eric pulled out the phone that Henry used to communicate with him. He texted, "Had to tell my wife your name."

He followed up quickly with, "Nothing else." Sweat broke out on his brow. The phone felt slippery in his hand. He put it in his pocket. He couldn't just stand there and wait for a response for hours. That would be crazy.

It buzzed almost immediately and he yanked it out, typed in his unlock code. The response surprised him. "That shouldn't be a problem. Make sure you bring her to New York. It's time I met your wife."

CHAPTER 3

Mr. Parks visited Mimi every day. Was he cheering her up or just tiring her out? He didn't know. He could wrangle business people so easily, but he found doctors and nurses to be puzzling. But then again, he knew, they were puzzled too. He looked for ways to cheer Mimi up. He came in one afternoon with a bag full of multivitamins and fish oil.

Mimi smiled. "This isn't like you!"

"I looked it up. Okay, well, Margaret looked it up. She's into vitamins."

"And she looks great," said Mimi half encouraging, half teasing. She often teased her father about his beautiful and obsessively healthy, marathon-running secretary.

"Well, she said you should see her herbalist as well, but only if you want to, sweetheart."

"Sure, it can't hurt. Is this lady discreet?"

"The best, according to Margaret."

"I don't want to end up accidentally becoming the spokesperson for lavender oil or flaxseeds or whatever it is they prescribe."

He laughed. "I'm going to start taking the fish oil too. She got me a bottle. You've been telling me for years to do something to protect my skin," he said.

"Right, I completely believe that you will remember to do that." She laughed a big, real, open laugh. The sound was so sweet to him; he was overjoyed that he had thought to buy the vitamins. He would have taken castor oil just to hear her laugh at him. She was sitting up in bed and looked more energized than before. The doctors had told them that she would get more accustomed to the seizures, in a way get stronger, be less tired afterward. Even the tingling, the strange sensations, she would come to understand those, not to panic.

"When you're ready for them, Margaret has an overwhelming number of suggestions for you, and for me. She wrote them down. I think there's even a feng shui consultant in there somewhere. She says this woman is the best in LA for making your house promote health and tranquility."

"Who doesn't want health and tranquility? I'm guessing *that* suggestion was really for you. But don't hire her because we are not updating the '70s spaceship kitchen, ever," Mimi teased. "Don't even try to get me to do that." Mimi remembered when she was sixteen and had asked him to update the house. He had done a few cosmetic things but nothing to the dark, wood-trimmed, '70s interior. He loved the safe, cozy feel of it. Compared with everyone else's mansion, at the Parks' house you felt like you were in a real house. Mr. Parks didn't want a house in which the ceilings were high enough that they could harbor birds of prey, didn't want a house in which you could get lost. When Mimi and Paloma were little, he loved that he could sit in the living room and always hear where they were, their little feet tromping around, their games.

"I won't touch it. The orange spaceship stays," he said, enjoying her banter.

"What else does Margaret want me to do?" asked Mimi.

"Yoga."

"Maybe," an impish grin came over her face, "if you do it too!"

"What?"

"Don't you want me to get better?"

"That's not fair!" He laughed.

"What? Me using my illness to manipulate you? It's totally fair."

"Is not!"

"It's practical from my point of view. You've always said to use the tools you have. Because of my illness, you might live forever!"

"I don't know how to feel about that."

"You'll feel better about it once you've taken a bunch of fish oil and yoga."

Mr. Parks prepared his rebuttal but stopped mid-thought as he looked at Mimi. She was looking over his shoulder and her face fell. He turned to see a doctor, one they hadn't met yet, with a clipboard and a very forced smile.

"Miss Parks. Good news; we can let you go home tomorrow!"

Mimi didn't know what to say. *Was* that good news? They were going to discharge her with no real diagnosis? That was it? They had nothing for her? Mr. Parks read her mind.

"How can you discharge her if you don't even know what's wrong?" Mr. Parks felt fury rising in his throat. "She's having a seizure or two every day."

"Well," the doctor's voice was practical, sensible, impartial but also nervous. Mr. Parks had to remind himself that doctors are people too. The doctor continued, "She's not improving here. She can't stay here forever. To be perfectly honest, we've done everything we can do in the hospital context. She didn't respond to the most common anti-seizure medications. Her care will have to be managed by a neurologist who can try different medications, combinations of medications. Dr. Betts does see patients outside the hospital. Or you can choose someone else. She may need more testing, but there's no reason for her to stay here for that. She may see some improvement from just being at home where she can get better sleep and be surrounded by familiar things. She does need to be very careful about falling." The doctor handed him some papers and a pamphlet titled "My Seizures." It fell open to reveal pictures of multiracial people smiling. Mr. Parks couldn't remember the last time anyone had handed him a pamphlet. He thought the world had moved far beyond pamphlets. Were there really only three pages of information about seizures to be learned? Where was the flash drive full of information, and the eager interns? Where were the multiple proposals for him to choose from, the pie charts? Where was the boardroom?

He took a breath and tried to take stock of the situation. Mimi would see the best neurologist. He would get her a nurse. She would be happier at home, with Martine. He turned to Mimi. "I'll phone Martine and let her know. She will be thrilled."

Mimi wanted to go home. But she wanted to go home healthy. She wanted to go back to her life. If she went home sick, did that mean they were giving up? She wanted to get up in the morning and sail down the stairs to her espresso machine while fielding phone calls about promotional ads and appearances. She wanted to slip into the pool and let the world melt away. She figured that was not going to be an option. She had yet to research swimming with epilepsy, but she didn't think she should get her hopes up.

Mr. Parks called Martine.

"Yes, tomorrow, they're letting her come home tomorrow."

"Oh, Mr. Parks! Muchas gracias!" Martine sounded so relieved on the phone that that he felt relieved too. He halfway listened to Martine's plans for what she was going to cook and how she was going to make Mimi safe and happy. He watched his daughter out of the corner of his eye and could tell that she was terrified. He was terrified too. What if this was going to be their new forever?

The next morning he stood by the door waiting for Mimi to change into the clothes he had brought. She was so fashionable, even in her casual, leaving-the-hospital wear. She had given him very specific instructions on where to find the right oversized shirt, which ballet flats. He stood in the hall and marveled at her attention to detail. Maybe he hadn't given her chosen career enough credit. The hospital counselor approached him. He recognized her from Mimi's disparaging description, the precision of her hairstyle, the protrusion of her elbows. She was skinny even by LA standards and weaving side to side like a skittish animal. He tried to ignore her until it was embarrassingly obvious that she was approaching him.

Finally he said, "Yes?"

"I heard you're taking Mimi home today."

"Yes, the doctors feel it's best."

"You know she's despondent. She may be depressed."

"Well, she suddenly started having seizures and there doesn't seem to be any reason for it. Also I don't know why we haven't found the medication that controls it yet." His frustration was measured, but formidable. He wanted this woman to go away.

The counselor continued, "It's particularly hard to be sick when you're famous."

Mr. Parks was rattled. He hadn't expected to have to have a conversation about fame. It felt vulgar to him.

"Being famous gives you a feeling of invincibility. People think being famous makes your life easy, but, in some specific ways, it makes life very difficult. To have a chronic illness…"

"We don't know that this will be chronic," he snapped.

"No, we don't. But it's worth thinking about. If you come out with it publicly you become the person who defines it. It's not just being sick, it's being sick for the whole world to see, or it's plummeting out of the spotlight. Some people channel the shock into doing something productive. It's okay if she doesn't want to do the show anymore, but try not to let her hide completely."

Her last words echoed in his ears. *Try not to let her hide completely.* He supposed it was possible to be both obnoxious and astute in her profession.

Mimi stared out the car window on the way home. Was it her imagination or was everything too bright, too clear? Her eyes were wet. She realized she had forgotten her sunglasses. They pulled up to the house. Mimi wondered what the feng shui expert would think of this low-lying house with large asymmetrical windows and cedar trim. When it was built, it was the nicest house in the neighborhood. Now it was the oldest. The angle of the roof sloped down in the back where the lawn also sloped away. This was one of the gentlest of the Beverly Hills. The long, single-story kitchen and living rooms made a sharp right angle into the two stories of bedrooms. All the bedrooms had their own french doors and small rectangular balconies, making the house look like a Lego hotel. Martine's suite was downstairs; Mimi's, her father's, and Paloma's rooms were upstairs. She saw that the blinds were drawn on her balcony in preparation for the hangover she was expecting to wake up with when she left the house more than a week ago. Mr. Parks drove slowly into the garage. The eight-car garage was the most extravagant thing on the property. They had moved in when Mimi was a baby; even though SkyCut was already a booming company, Mr. Parks was hesitant to buy something he thought was excessive. Since Mimi's mother left, they had only made two upgrades: the pool and the garage. Mr. Parks got out of the car and looked at her expectantly.

"I'll just be a minute," she said, and pulled out her phone. He didn't want to leave her there. They had told her to always walk with someone.

She understood the meaning of his hesitation. "It's all of a hundred feet," she said irritably. Mr. Parks walked into the house.

Mimi texted her agent, short and to the point, "Cancel all my contracts except the perfume."

The swift response came. "Has someone hacked your phone?" A few moments later, "Are you having a reality TV meltdown?"

"No," Mimi texted back. "I'm sick. Not drugs. Don't tell anyone, just cancel everything but the perfume."

A minute later Mimi wrote, "And start looking for other clients."

"Bastien will call you about 'Mimi does Europe'," her agent wrote back immediately. This was a woman whose phone was in her hand every second of every day. Mimi could almost hear the clipped tone of voice in her text, at the same time no-nonsense and slightly gossipy. It was true that Bastien wouldn't let her off the hook without talking to her. Better to get it over with.

"Fine."

He would call. She would tell him. He would let her off the hook for season two with a quick, "Okay, I'll come up with a plausible excuse." He was direct. He was busy. His world had already moved past her.

Mimi got out of the car and walked into the house. She ran her fingers along the front of her green vintage Jaguar. She didn't know if she would drive again. Don't cry, she thought, don't cry, and don't think about anything else you might never do again. Just don't think it. She opened the door to the house. Her father looked relieved even though it had been only a few minutes. Martine came up and gave her a big hug, then stepped back, smoothing back Mimi's hair with her gentle hands. Mimi felt like going to bed though it was eleven o'clock in the morning. She was faced with a terrifying thought: What am I going to do all day, every day, if I feel this bad? At least there was the television.

Where once she had enjoyed dramatic television, and foreign art movies, now she found she liked the Discovery Channel, anything with animals, and action movies with a lot of car chases; the more car chases the better. She tried listening to books on tape, but could only make it halfway through before shutting them off. Only Sherlock Holmes and Agatha Christie murder mysteries could hold her attention to the end. She best liked the ones where she already knew the plot.

Now that she was home, her eating, always difficult for her, waned to an all-time low. Half-eaten items started to pile up around her: half a sandwich, half a muffin, a half-opened yogurt container without a spoon.

Mr. Parks offered to hire her a nurse, but the truth was she only wanted to see Martine. Actually, she wanted to be completely alone, but they had warned her about falls. She stayed where Martine could see her; Martine, to her credit, didn't try to talk. She just cooked Mimi's favorite things, set them out to be eaten or not, sat by her when she showered, slept on the couch in Mimi's room.

Mr. Parks watched her glide around the house, like a ghost. It was agony for him. He was a doer. And what was he doing? He was watching his daughter disintegrate. He put off trip after trip. He was always traveling, but now he spent most of his time on the phone trying to avoid travel. But what's a business venture when you have a daughter? The biggest SkyCut event of the year was coming up in Oslo. Before Mimi got sick, he had been looking forward to it. It was shaping up to be a good year. He had even started to enjoy public speaking. Now he wasn't sure he could get out of it. He made plans to go, feeling guilty even though he wasn't sure that he was helping Mimi by being at home. She wouldn't even let him take her to her appointments with the neurologist and the herbalist; Dennis took her. Who could have guessed how useful having a driver would prove? Two days before Mr. Parks was supposed to leave for Oslo, he came and sat by Mimi, who was lying in a lounge chair by the pool. She didn't look up at him.

"I can cancel my trip," he said tentatively.

"Please don't. I'm okay." A gust of wind caused the water to lap the edge in soft waves.

"You know you can't go in the pool." He meant to say something sweet, but somehow the rules came out instead.

"Yes, or my car or anywhere with hard surfaces." She turned her face away from him.

"I'm sorry. We'll figure this out, honey."

"I know," said Mimi, but she knew they would not. She hadn't made any progress with the neurologist except to try some drugs that made her vomit, which did not help her eating. The neurologist had started weighing her, making clucking noises over the scale. She tried to wear her heaviest pants and belts when she went to his office. It was embarrassing.

Mr. Parks squinted into the sun and made a decision that he had been laying the groundwork for over the last couple of weeks. "I have something for you that I think you'll really like," he said. "I'll be back." As he walked away from her, he pulled out his cell phone, made a quick call, and said, "We're ready, now, if at all possible."

Mimi watched him leave and then went back to staring at the pool. What could he be talking about? She couldn't imagine anything that she would really like right now except maybe a miracle drug. She turned her e-reader on, and a slightly robotic British accent began to dictate

48

Sir Arthur Conan Doyle's "Sherlock Holmes: The Final Problem." She stared into space, trying to lose herself in the mechanical voice. She had downloaded this retro e-reader voice on purpose. She preferred the older e-reader voices, the ones that made mistakes. She always felt a little glee at their mispronunciations and a little pity for them. After all, they were just machines, trying their very best. She felt no pity for Sherlock Holmes, though. He was making foolish choices with his life. Why didn't he just go back to London and find some other way to kill Moriarty? She was looking forward to the part where he falls off the cliff. It's amazing, she thought, she used to hate sitting. She used to be busy all the time. Now her sore, exhausted body was glued to the lounge chair all day.

The e-reader droned on. Dr. Watson was too naïve, it was not believable. Someone who spent that much time with Sherlock Holmes wouldn't be so gullible. He would have learned something. The afternoon was hot and she wanted to get in the water, maybe even more so because she wasn't allowed. What if she just put her feet in? Maybe up to the knees? Her father had the pool put in when she was a child. She had gotten to pick it out. Of all the possible shapes, she chose this elaborate teardrop with a big staircase and attached Jacuzzi hot tub. It had been so fancy when it was new. Now everyone had something more exciting, but really, why bother? She couldn't believe that she was an adult and she was going to waste her twenties, maybe even her thirties and on into forever living a half-life, lying down. According to her e-reader,

Holmes was lost forever, and Watson felt sad. She didn't bother to close the app when it beeped at the end of the story. She dozed off.

Her father drove up an hour later; she heard the sound of his car on the drive and remembered he had gone to get something for her. He had left the gate open in the privacy fence of the patio when he left, and now he pulled right up to it. He got out of his car, and opened the back door as though he were a working valet. Mimi was so surprised at what she saw that she stood up without thinking. A pair of big brown eyes stared at her from the back seat, where a sleek gray dog was comfortably seated, his face calm, his ears alert.

"Okay, boy!" her father said awkwardly and made a sweeping gesture with his hand.

The dog jumped gracefully to the ground and stood by Mr. Parks.

For a moment Mimi completely forgot all of her problems. She ran up to them.

"Really? Really, for me? Oh, he's so cute! Daddy, he's CUTE! I thought you didn't want me to have a dog." She fondled his ears. They were unbelievably silky. He wagged his tail patiently. He had a wide chest. Mimi scratched him behind the ears and he leaned into her hand. She felt a swell of joy in her heart.

His fur was short and soft; she ran her hands along his back and patted his sides. His tail kept wagging.

"He's a seizure dog," said her father.

"Oh," she said. Her enthusiasm for the dog suddenly drained out of her.

Mr. Parks saw her smile fall. "Just try him, please. With his trainer he was a hundred percent effective."

"Oh." She stopped patting the dog's head and her hands fell listless at her sides.

"The head of the program actually said he'd never seen anything like him. He's not just accurate; he's so calm. I don't…" Mr. Parks looked at Mimi's crestfallen face. "You don't have to take him, honey. I just thought… because you've been…he can help you. Service dogs are allowed everywhere now. He can even go out with you, if he works well, when you go out with your friends."

"I don't want to go out with my friends."

Her father searched for words, "Then he can…sit with you."

She looked at the dog, who sat quietly, ears alert as though he understood their words. "Did he come with a name?" she asked.

"Ky," said her father.

"When I wanted a dog a couple of years ago I was going to get a Husky/Pomeranian mix puppy and name him Thor. They look like tiny, tiny Huskies and I was going to put him in a carrier and take him everywhere." Her voice took on a note of hysteria. "Everyone was going to love him because he was so little."

"You can change his name," Mr. Parks said, gesturing to the dog, trying to calm her agitation.

The gray dog pushed his head gently back under Mimi's hand. Surprised, she pulled her hand away.

"I like Ky, I guess." She looked back and forth between Ky and her father as though they were teaming up against her. "I just hate everything else! I don't want the dog, I don't want the seizures, I want to do my show! I want to get in the pool! I want to drive! I hate being sick, I hate it, I hate it, I hate it, I HATE it!" Her tears started flowing freely, but she could hardly feel them running down her face. The heat of her tears matched perfectly with the heat of the afternoon. She knew she should be embarrassed to cry in front of her father, but she was too frustrated and disappointed to care. "I don't want THIS to be my life!"

Mr. Parks looked at her helplessly. A year ago he would have wished that Mimi would take her life seriously; now he realized he'd give anything to watch her walk out the door as she was before, careless, chaotic, young, sporting a new dress. He wished he'd gotten her the pocketbook Husky that she had wanted.

Ky was motionless, but his eyes were on Mimi.

Mr. Parks left for Oslo. Ky's trainer from the Seizure Dog Center came to the house every day for a week. They went over possible seizure alert behaviors. They also practiced regular dog training: sit, stay, come. But the training turned out to be just a formality.

"He never misses," said the trainer.

And it was true. Patient, insistent, he was always by her side. He never pulled the leash. He never snatched a treat. He sat down in front of her ten minutes before every seizure and gave a gentle bark as if to say, "You cannot pass this way yet. You have something you have to do."

Mimi asked the trainer if all the dogs were that good.

"They're not all that good around the house," he laughed. "Some of them come with regular dog behaviors, stealing food off the counters, chasing squirrels, stuff like that. One of our families has to hide all their socks and shoes from their alert dog."

"Oh, I'm so glad that's not me! I know it's a stereotype but, as you can imagine, I have a lot of shoes."

He shrugged. "It's your job."

"Was," she corrected.

He reached out a hand and patted her on the back with the most sympathy and camaraderie she had ever felt from another human being. Mimi admired his ease in talking about seizures.

He continued, "All of our dogs excel at seizure alert. They have to. Otherwise it would be dangerous to have them. But what's interesting about Ky is that his timing seems to be perfect; you could set a clock by him. Not all of our dogs are like that."

"Yes," said Mimi, "always exactly ten minutes."

"And I know you said he's just as good when I'm not here, even at night," said the trainer, impressed.

"Yeah," said Mimi. "It has only happened once, but he barked to wake me up so that I could put in my bite stick, ten minutes exactly. And you know what's crazy? I feel like he's so familiar. I recognize him somehow, from somewhere. I recognize his eyes."

"Well that's common with seizures, that sense of déja vu. They didn't tell you about that in the hospital?"

"They didn't tell me much at the hospital."

"Well, déja vu and seizures have been reported together forever, not for everyone, obviously, but for some. It's not even culturally specific. It's the same feeling all over the world."

"Yeah, but I don't think that's it," said Mimi. "I mean, it's not a situation I re-live. It's his eyes, his face that I recognize. Plus, I don't have déja vu about anything else."

"Seizure feelings are hard to explain. I definitely feel that my dog is familiar, but I've had him for a long time. Still, there is something odd about Ky. He came to us just a few weeks ago, and he's already more than ready to go into service. When your father came to get him, it was as if he was ready to go. It was like none of the other dogs was even an option. I felt that way too. Now I can't quite think why."

Ky cocked his head at them and exhaled, like a sigh.

"Sometimes his gestures are so human," Mimi laughed.

With Ky around, Mimi started to regain confidence. She could walk around the house and yard without holding onto someone's arm. She started to have fewer seizures. She was elated the first time twenty-four hours went by without a seizure. The trainer said that was a known side effect of the dogs.

"Doctors think it's because they reduce stress," he said. "Who knows what it is, really? It's pretty amazing that dogs can sense seizures when we can't at all."

"You know what I think it is? I think the dog makes you feel like you're not going to die. I mean, I know you're not likely to die from seizures. I've read the statistics. A long seizure that you never wake up from, that's so unlikely. But when it's *you,* you think, I could die, like, there's something special about me, and not special in a good way. Like sometimes when you get on a plane and you know in your mind that people don't mostly die on planes but you think, *I* could. That could happen to *me* right now. But the dog makes you think, oh, right, this is normal. Okay buddy, I'll be here when you wake up. And I'll be the same."

"The dog definitely always feels that you're going to come out the other side," the trainer agreed.

"And hopefully he's right." Mimi sighed dubiously. They had come out to the lawn to go over sit, stay, come. Ky always got it right, so they were practicing heel without a lead, just walking around the yard.

"Are you in a support group, Mimi?"

"No. I see a neurologist and an herbalist. I might start seeing a counselor or a hypnotist or an acupuncturist or a feng shui consultant," she laughed. "Those are just a few of the suggestions I'm considering."

"At least you're considering all your options," he acknowledged with a grin. "Isn't feng shui interior design?"

"People who do it would say it's more than that, but, yes, sort of."

"How would that help?"

"Who knows? Therefore, there's no reason not to try it." Mimi smiled. "But right now I'm trying to just add one thing at a time."

"Support groups are really helpful."

"Right, but then all it takes is one indiscreet person."

"I know. Your life has some special considerations. But think about it."

"I will."

"There really is nothing quite like people who understand exactly what you're going through."

"I believe it. I didn't realize how lonely I was before Ky showed up, you and Ky. It's like other people just made me feel lonelier."

"I've always had seizures," said the trainer, "never had a time in my life without them. I think it's probably easier that way."

"I never thought about it. Never once in my life did it occur to me that I could start having seizures. Honestly, it never occurred to me that I could get sick at all. I was stupid, pompous, naïve, and...did I say stupid?"

"I think that's pretty normal."

"To be stupid, pompous, and naïve?"

The trainer laughed. "Yes. I think *that* is normal. But it's also normal to not even wonder what other people's lives are like, or to imagine that you could be different."

"I wondered what people's lives in other countries were like."

"Naturally; that's how you ended up with your show."

"And I wondered what people's lives were like who were watching the show sometimes. I actually had this daydream that I would switch sides of the television, that I would end up in a doublewide trailer somewhere in

Middle America watching 'Mimi Does Europe.' In case you're wondering, fake me admired real me, in the daydream." She looked down at her hands. "Sorry, that probably sounded really pompous. Maybe all those people in Middle America just watch because there's nothing good on TV. I guess I am pompous, but that's not what I meant about the daydream. I meant...I just want to know what the other side of the TV is like."

"Now see," said the trainer cheerfully, "I never wondered what that would be like."

"What?"

"To be on television, to have millions of people know your face and your name."

"You never wondered that?"

"I don't think so. I just watch television, I don't think about making it."

"I took for granted that everyone wants to be famous."

"I grew up as a sick kid. I just wanted to be normal."

"You're more normal than I am," said Mimi. "I mean, kind of, that came out wrong."

"I'm over it, wanting to be normal. Well, I'm almost over it." There was a rawness to his words.

Ky licked the trainer's hand appreciatively. Mimi had almost forgotten he was there.

"He's such a good dog," said the trainer. "You lucked out."

Martine watched them out the window, strolling through the grass. She was hopeful. Martine felt as if the dog was real medicine. Plus, she liked having him around. She liked feeding him. Dogs were so appreciative of food, much more appreciative than young women who had to make a living in Hollywood, she thought. Martine had worked for Mr. Parks for twenty years and they had never had a dog, even though Mimi had wanted one. Mimi had begged for one, but Mr. Parks said no, they traveled too much to get a dog. And, Martine thought, a puppy is a lot of work. When the girls were young, he was also probably trying to protect Martine from having to work too much. She appreciated that. Watching Mimi walk so comfortably with Ky was one of those ironic twists of fate, she thought. You never really get what you want in the way you want it.

After Ky had been with them for a week, Mimi had a terrible night, seizure after seizure. Ky sat at the foot of her bed all night. Every time she went to get up he gave a warning bark. Martine made soft cooing noises over her when she regained consciousness, got her water, turned her on her side. The next morning Mimi watched the sun rise pale and watery over the hills as if it too was struggling to come up for air. Bleary, confused and exhausted, she took coffee in her bed. She drank it black.

"I can't even face a latte," she said miserably. "How come you are so great, Martine? I know you didn't sleep at all."

"Mothers don't always need sleep, querida," said Martine.

"It's like I'm becoming a little kid again."

"No, my heart, it's like you're really becoming an adult. But I still wish it away for you."

Mimi spent the day in bed. Martine brought her cheese sandwiches. Ky sat and looked at her. She looked into those deep, dark eyes that she swore she recognized. She thought either he was plotting to destroy her, or he really wanted a cheese sandwich. She gave him a cheese sandwich. For a dog, he was a tidy eater.

"Don't start begging, though," she told him. "I don't want you to be a bad dog." She could have sworn he raised his eyebrows at her. She thought about how she used to lie in bed with a hangover. What a waste of time, and health.

That night she asked Martine to go back to her own room.

"I have Ky," she said. "Unless he warns me, I really want to be alone."

Mimi curled up under the covers, her face toward the windows and the pale orange California night. Every muscle and nerve in her body felt as though it had reached its limit.

"Ky, I'm glad you're here." She spoke without looking at him. "I don't know what I'd do if you hadn't shown up." She paused long enough that the dog settled his head on his paws, thinking she was asleep, but then she continued in a soft voice, "I know it's stupid but I thought the world wanted me, needed me. I thought I was important. I thought I was destined for greatness, all kinds of greatness, fame and fortune and a healthy, happy little family with some hot husband. I know that makes me sound ungrateful. I was just lucky, I guess, and now I'm just unlucky. Or maybe it's really like they say and you create everything in your life by thinking about it, the whole 'law of attraction' thing. But I don't know how I created this." She winced, trying to arrange her sore shoulders underneath her so that she could get comfortable. She felt as though even the marrow of her bones was sore. "You know what I am now? I'm the antelope that gets eaten by the lion, the one that can't quite keep up, the one the announcer talks about on the nature channel. The one where he's like, 'Oh, you don't have to feel bad for that antelope, it was sick anyway, a lion's gotta eat!' Does it matter that I don't want to be that one? I want to be the girl I was before." She sighed deeply. "Except not exactly. I want to be that girl except I want to remember this feeling, so I don't take anything for granted anymore. I don't want to be left behind." She fell asleep with tears sliding across her nose onto her pillow.

Ky stood up and shook himself, then paced for a few moments at the foot of the bed. He hadn't changed for a long time, too long. He could tell because he was starting to feel restless and, despite the momentous decisions before him, his mind kept reverting to the several boxes of treats Martine kept in the pantry. He rounded the corner of the bed and looked at Mimi's face. She was really asleep. The tears had stopped and her breathing was rhythmic.

Ky stopped pacing; in a moment, the figure of a man had taken his place.

The transformation was so quick and so quiet it was as though it hadn't happened at all. He looked at Mimi thoughtfully and then sat down in the easy chair that faced her bed. He knit his hands together tightly. He needed to think the way a human thinks. Mimi shifted and sighed. Asleep, she looked young, healthy, unblemished. He sat through the night looking out the window, looking at Mimi. He couldn't wait out the safer course of action much longer. Just before dawn he returned to the floor, changed back into the dog, and fell asleep. Ky thought he might make a radical decision, but not today.

CHAPTER 4

In the morning Ky was stretched out at the foot of Mimi's bed as usual. They had slept in, and the sun was high in the sky by the time they came down to breakfast. Martine was sitting at the breakfast table with a cup of coffee listening to the Spanish news on the radio through her phone. She got up as they came down.

"Mail came for you, querida," she said. Martine handed over the envelope with some trepidation. It was an invitation to a yearly charity gala. Mimi had forgotten that it was coming up. Ky was expecting it.

Martine wondered if there was something she could say to try to convince Mimi to go to the annual gala for world refugees that Henry was hosting. She didn't actually approve of Henry, but given the circumstances, she thought if she could get Mimi to go anywhere, it would be good for her. Mimi glanced at it, and then let the pretty linen invitation fall from her hand into the trash.

As Mimi walked away, Ky looked over at Martine to make sure she wasn't watching, then fished it out.

All day Mimi's phone rang and rang. She put it on vibrate only. Then she moved it to the foot of her lounge chair. She threw her sweater over it, and then a towel, but she could still hear it. Finally, she picked it up and flung it toward the pool. Ky got up quickly, made a flying leap, and, before it reached the water, caught the phone in midair. He landed on the patio and brought it back to her, tail wagging.

"Fine," she said as she took the phone. "Everyone else is after me, why not you too? It just figures that before I got sick everyone wanted me to do something serious and stop having a social life." She scowled at the water. "Careful what you wish for, you know?"

Was it her imagination, or did he nod in sympathy?

"You're a weird dog, you know that?"

Ky wagged his tail. She could have sworn he was laughing at his own private joke. He lay down next to her and his wagging tail thumped into her ankle. She couldn't decide if she liked the feeling, or if it was irritating. "A weird dog, that's exactly what I meant." His tail wagged harder.

Mimi got into bed that night in a foul mood and pulled the covers up over her head. She had had navy blue sheets, always had, since she was a kid. She found them comforting, like climbing into the warm ocean. They blocked the light, and she needed to block out the world just now. She pulled the sheet tight around her ears and counted backwards from one hundred, a simple but effective trick. Martine had taught it to her so she always

63

counted in Spanish. "Cien, noventa y nueve, noventa y ocho…"

Ky sighed. He listened to her counting. He was loath to break the peace of the evening, but it was now or never. If she couldn't help him, or didn't believe him, he couldn't miss this opportunity. He was running out of time.

"…treinta y cinco, treinta y cuatro–"

Just as Mimi was dozing off she heard a man's voice, soft but resolved.

"Mimi. Mimi, I need your help."

Mimi bolted upright and pulled the sheets back to see a strange man standing at the foot of her bed. She screamed.

"I'm not sure how else to ask for it," Ky said quietly. "I've never been in this situation before. But I do. I need your help."

"Get away from me! Who are you?" Still in bed, she pushed herself back and pressed herself to the headboard, as far away from him as she could get.

"Please." Ky put his hands up in a gesture of supplication. "I'm not going to hurt you."

"What? What are you talking about? Who are you?"

"I was hoping I wouldn't have to tell you. I had a plan that was better, less intrusive." Ky turned back into a dog. The seamlessness, gracefulness of the motion shocked her as much as the transformation. The dog was unmistakably the man, and vice versa.

Martine's footsteps came running down the hall. She knocked frantically on the door. "Mimi, are you okay?

What happened? I'm coming in." Martine opened the door.

Ky the dog sat patiently at the foot of the bed. He kept his gaze fixed steadily on Mimi. She gazed back, wondering if she had just recovered from a hallucination, or had been dreaming. There was her dog on the floor, but his eyes said otherwise.

"I think– I think I had a nightmare. I think I'm okay," Mimi said slowly.

"Do you want me to stay with you?" Martine sat on the bed and instinctively put her hand on Mimi's forehead. "You don't feel warm, but you look flushed."

"No, I'll be okay."

Martine kissed her on the top of her head. "Do you need anything? Absolutely anything? Let me get you something, querida. Hot cocoa, cold cocoa?"

Mimi laughed. "Tempting, but no."

"Anything at all?"

"Don't worry. I'll call you if I need you. I promise."

"Okay, honey."

Martine got up and walked quietly to the door. She turned and gave Mimi a big air kiss, then softly clicked the door closed behind her. Ky and Mimi looked at each other for a long moment, long enough for her to doubt what she had seen, and then Ky stood up and took human form in a single perfect movement, never losing eye contact.

"Who are you?" she gasped.

"I am an Or-ta, something you might call a shapeshifter, a trickster."

"I wasn't paying that much attention in biology class, but I'm pretty sure that's not a real thing."

"How about old English literature? Native American history? Greek mythology?" he asked.

"No dog-men that I remember."

A half-smile crossed Ky's face. "We're not just dog-men. We take a shape that is correct to the world we're in, correct to the circumstances we're in. Earth is full of shapes, and I can recreate a handful of them. But I can still also use some magic, some of the tools of my world. And, as you see, I can change."

"Am I dreaming? I'm dreaming. This isn't real. Is this real?"

"I am Ky. Ky the dog is really a dog but also me, if that makes sense."

"It doesn't."

"I can take many different shapes."

"Why are you here?"

"I guess I'm here as a..." he hesitated, searching for a good word. "Spy," he finally concluded.

"Spying on me?"

"No, but I need your help." He sat down in her puffy pink velvet easy chair. He was too tall for it, she noticed. His knees stuck up. He looked out of place in her very female bedroom. He furrowed his brow. She had seen Ky the dog make the same expression, as though he was deeply concerned.

"You need my help to be a spy?"

"I need your help to spy on someone at the gala for world refugees. You got the invitation today. I need you to go. I need you to be your old self, to a certain extent. And I need you to bring me, at least past the gate."

"You're a spy so you need me to go to a party? That doesn't make any sense."

Ky smiled. "Spies are always going to parties in those movies that you watch, the ones with the hero who says his name twice."

"James Bond."

"He goes to parties."

"I didn't think that was a real thing."

"Well, what about Mata Hari?"

"Who's Mata Hari?"

"You don't know about Mata Hari? I didn't think that was that long ago." His brow furrowed deeper. "Regardless, this party lends itself to my purposes."

"Who are you spying on?"

Ky hesitated for a long moment. Here he was faced with the second radical decision of the night. How could he trust Mimi? She was barely an adult of her race, spoiled, chaotic. With the truth, she could reveal his presence before he was ready to make his move. She could put herself in danger. She could put him in danger. But wasn't everyone more dangerous without the truth? Had he not learned that the last time he had been on Earth?

"I believe you think his name is Henry Halstead"

"Henry?"

"Henry is a, hmmm, crook? An imposter." Ky realized how long it was since he had spoken to a person.

He knew his speech sounded outdated. He would work on it.

"He is kind of my boyfriend," said Mimi.

"I know that."

"So you have been spying on me."

"I was sent to find out what Henry's plans are. I suppose you could say I spied on all of his close acquaintances."

"I thought you were from the Seizure Dog Center."

"My apologies. I didn't have a lot of options."

"What did he do?"

"I don't know yet. All I know is that he's cultivating friends who are powerful in your political and social system. Seeking out power in your world is forbidden to us. He has been pretending to be human for a long time."

Mimi sputtered, "Pretending to be human?" Her mind turned to the nights that she had spent with Henry and she shook a little. She couldn't help it. She didn't believe what Ky was telling her, or did she?

"Henry is of my race, a trickster."

"No, he can't be," she said defensively. "I mean, I've never seen him change into a dog!"

"I don't know if he has a dog shape," Ky replied thoughtfully. "Regardless, up until tonight you'd never seen me as anything else. We don't reveal ourselves anymore, not without great need."

"Why do you need my help?"

"I can't get over the threshold of his house without an invitation."

"Like a vampire?"

"Not exactly, no; more because Henry's house is under a lot of security, both human and Or-ta. It will be somewhat fragmented the night of the party, but I still need you to cross, so that I can cross. I need to be your invitee, so that I won't…" He thought about how to explain this. "So that I won't cast a shadow on his security system. He also likes you. If you go, he will be very much engaged in the pleasure of the event."

"So that way you can spy on him? I'll distract him with how cute I am, and you can snoop around his house?"

"Essentially, yes." He paused, calmly meeting her skeptical gaze. "Will you go?"

"I haven't been anywhere since…" Then a thought occurred to her. Her voice suddenly rose. "Did you…is it your fault that I got sick? Or Henry's?" Her mind flew wildly to the possibilities. She had seen Henry the day of her first seizure. Had she been subjected to some kind of magic?

"No, I don't have that kind of power." Ky's voice was calm, but sympathetic. "Henry is much older than I am. He might have that kind of power, but I don't see how it would help him. Until your illness, he was using you to get to powerful people, entertainers like you. And he has been trying to reach you."

"Yes."

"But you've been ignoring him."

"And everyone else."

"I don't think he would have done it. It wouldn't help him."

"And you, you didn't, like, cast a spell on me or anything?"

"No. It may seem like a strange coincidence to you, but as far as I can tell, your illness is of your world only. I am sorry. I was looking for an opportunity to get to Henry, looking at all his close acquaintances. The others are... well, let's just say that they have a very strong incentive to protect him. You, you're independent. He needed you more than you needed him, clearly, more than you wanted him. I would have tried something else, but when you got sick, I saw that I could enter your world. The dog is a convenient form for me, good hearing, great sense of smell, uncanny ability to recognize bad intentions. Our powers are increased by our form. It was a great opportunity. I would have had a harder time winning your trust some other way, especially since you've been... isolated."

"You did have my trust," she said quietly.

"Now, I hope to earn it again. I know it will be different." The soft glow of the night sky illuminated his lanky seated frame. He looked human, but not quite.

Mimi's mind was racing. She had so many questions she could hardly think of one to start with, except maybe the one that mattered most to her, "And so, then, can you..." She paused trying to figure out what and exactly how she wanted to say it, but he finished her thought for her.

"I can't heal you, no."

"Not even as a reward, if I really help you out?"

"I would do it, Mimi. If that were in my power I would have done it already. It would have saved us this conversation, and I know you suffer. I have seen it."

She looked down, realizing that a total stranger had seen her most vulnerable moments.

He continued, "All the worlds have curses, blights. Illness is one of yours."

She turned that disappointment over in her mind for a few moments. "I can't go. What if I go and I'm a mess all night?"

"For the gala I can tell you if you'll have any seizures. We can plan the whole night around them."

"You get more than a ten-minute warning?"

"I get about a day depending on the circumstances."

"Why didn't you say so before? That would have been very helpful!" She laughed.

His eyes twinkled. "Up until now, we didn't have that kind of relationship."

"The kind where you're also a person?"

"Yes, that kind."

"And you're an…"

"Or-ta."

She rolled the word around in her mouth. It suited the man, and the dog. "Why should I believe you about Henry?"

Ky thought for a moment. "Martine doesn't like him," he said, hoping that would be enough.

Mimi laughed. "She does have good people instincts. On the other hand, she thinks you're a dog."

"I am! Tell me something you know about Henry, something he has told you. Did he grow up somewhere, have a family? How old is he? Where did he get his money?"

Mimi realized that in all their conversations Henry hadn't been forthcoming about his personal life. "I don't know. I don't know any of that. But that doesn't mean he's bad. I mean, he could be like you, but he could be the good guy. How do I know he's the bad guy and you're the good guy?"

"Always a good question, but really, I think you should believe me because I'm telling the truth." The power of his voice increased suddenly, not the volume, but some kind of force behind it. "I don't always, but now I am." Mimi looked at him. He was impossible not to believe; maybe it was the steadiness of his gaze. It was as though he really had cast a spell on her, and she recognized the power. It was a power that Henry had as well. She had felt so lucky to be with Henry because he was special, different from everyone else, more sure of himself, more commanding. She had never seen him speak to someone and not get immediate, rapt attention. There was an otherworldly magnetism that attracted everyone to Henry. Suddenly, that made sense.

She thought back on her relationship with Henry. "I was crazy about him. He is nice, super-charming, but creepy or disorienting, I guess. He's a very exciting person."

"I can see how that would be. He is powerful, even among Or-ta. That's why I didn't think you'd lose interest in him."

"I guess I've lost interest in almost everything."

"In a way, that shows strength on your part. Although, you already know that in the long run, there's no hiding from life."

"Don't you start on me too!"

"I've already started on you."

"Like when you caught my phone?" She laughed. "I should have known that was completely not normal."

"You did know. In a way, Martine knows too. Humans know much more than they're willing to believe in."

"Speaking of which, you'd better not disappear on me. I don't want another diagnosis in my medical chart that goes something like 'super-crazy delusions, thinks her dog is a person.'"

"You'll help me?"

"If Henry's not doing anything wrong, you'll leave him alone, right?" The words sounded lame to her as she said them. Thinking back on Henry in this new light, it was as if his actions started to make sense, his political friends, the entertainers that he "admired" that he had asked Mimi to introduce him to, even the places he went on vacation seemed slightly out of the ordinary. She didn't know why she hadn't seen it before. His desires were calculated to a specific end, but what?

"I would like nothing better."

They sat in silence, both gazing out at the night. Ky felt it had gone well, as well as could be hoped. He was now on treacherous territory until he had Henry in hand. Humans could be volatile. The last time he had become close to a real human, he had put his whole world in danger. He grimaced and tried to put the thought out of his mind. But, he considered, Mimi was different. She had a certain clarity under that thick veneer of pop culture. She only had to get him close to Henry. And she was his best shot. Outside the window a few stars were making an unusual appearance in the hazy sky. The room felt still, silent. Mimi was still pressed up against the elaborate headboard of her bed. The mahogany slats were cold. She felt small in that sea of cushions and fabric. But Ky had made no threatening moves. He sat still in her fluffy easy chair. If anything, she felt as if he had made himself vulnerable to her.

"You won't have any seizures tonight, Mimi, if you want to sleep," he said quietly.

And suddenly she did want to sleep. But despite her brave words, she wasn't sure if she wanted to wake up in the morning to Ky the dog or Ky the shapeshifter.

"I don't even know you," she said tiredly. "How can I sleep?"

"If I wanted to hurt you, I could have done so already," he said. "Plus, what makes you think that you could know me better as a person than as a dog? I'm just as much one as the other."

"So this isn't the real you?"

"This is not the shape in which I was born, no. But it's one I like. They all have their advantages. For example, sleep comes easier to a dog. Here, I'll go first." A slight smile played around his mouth, and with that he transformed back into a dog and lay down at the foot of her bed where he always slept, tucking his nose under his front two paws. His ears fell, relaxed. He let out a long sigh. He looked so sweet lying there, just a tired dog without secrets. Mimi relaxed a little bit and then curled up. He was right, of course: he clearly did not want to hurt her. She wondered, when you find out that the world is completely other than—or more than you thought—when, after that, is the right time to sleep?

Mimi slept deeply. When she awoke in the morning, she said nothing to Ky. She was waiting for him to say something, or do something so that she would know that she had not been dreaming. She noticed that he averted his gaze as she was dressing. Had he always done that? She couldn't remember. Why would she have cared? She came down to breakfast followed by Ky as usual, the soft thump of his paws down the stairs. She tried to behave normally, but she felt like she was suddenly walking around on another planet. She kept glancing at him. He met her gaze with those steady eyes, not quite a dog's eyes. She couldn't believe that she hadn't recognized it before. Martine was surprised when Mimi went to feed Ky and then turned to her.

"Do you think Ky can have huevos?"

Martine had grown up in rural El Salvador where there were dogs, but no grocery stores, and certainly no dog food. Martine laughed. "I never met a dog that didn't like huevos. He probably also wants a waffle." Huevos and waffles were a favorite breakfast in the Parks household.

Ky wagged his tail and went to lie down at Martine's feet.

"Your trainer would not approve," Martine said cheerfully as she laid out a human breakfast for Ky.

"I think he doesn't need to know about this one," said Mimi laughing.

Martine was surprised to see Mimi finish her breakfast, but as an experienced mother of girls, she said nothing. When Mimi told her that she was going to Henry's party she couldn't restrain herself. "Bueno querida, enjoy yourself some!"

"Martine, do you like Henry?"

Martine looked at her carefully, "Sure. He seems like a nice man."

"But you don't like him, do you?"

"No, he seems very, hmmm, tricky?" Mimi almost burst out laughing at Martine's choice of words. But she quickly followed with, "but don't miss the party."

Mimi smiled. "I won't."

Ky followed Mimi outside to lie in the lounge chair by the pool with her latte. It was their routine. Every day they lay by the pool, listened to books on tape or watched movies. Today, conveniently for Mimi, it would give her the chance to ask the hundreds of questions that had been circling through her head during breakfast.

76

"Can you speak as a dog?" Mimi asked as soon as they were out of Martine's earshot.

"Yes. Sometimes it's hard to remember not to." Ky was taking his usual place beside her. She looked at his face as he spoke; his lips barely moved, but the voice was that of Ky the man.

"That's strange. Dogs can't talk, you know."

"It's a trick," said Ky apologetically. "We cultivate our shapes over time so it's not too hard to work in some cross-characteristics. It's convenient. In this case, I used the human vocal chords, but the resonating cavity is magical. Sound is easy to change with magic because it always has some magical characteristics. Even untrained, non-magical beings can stumble across them, especially when singing, or, for example, playing the guitar. But for me, in my nonhuman shapes, I manipulate sound with magic so that I always have the same voice. That way I can hear myself and not be surprised."

Mimi just stared at his furry gray face, not entirely sure what he was talking about.

"Thanks for the waffle," he said quietly.

"Oh right, better than dog food?"

"Your housekeeper buys excellent dog food."

"Oh, sorry. It just felt weird."

"Not a problem. Dog food is delicious to a dog, but waffles are delicious to everyone. Given the choice, I would always take the huevos con waffles."

"There will be enchiladas for dinner."

"Excellent, if you don't think she'll get suspicious."

"Suspicious of what? That you're not a dog?"

"Good point. I love enchiladas." He stared out over the perfectly manicured landscaping. "I was worried that you would wake up in the morning and second-guess last night."

"Of course I second-guessed last night. I'm still second-guessing it!"

"It's been a long time since an Or-ta revealed his true nature to a human. I wasn't sure how to go about it."

"Maybe appearing in my bedroom as a strange man wasn't the best choice."

"I thought about that. Would just talking to you as a dog have been better?"

Mimi gave that a moment's thought, and then laughed. "No, no not better."

"I don't understand humans. In my human form, I feel as a human does, some things, anyway, and I have some human emotions, experiences. Sometimes I have to change shapes just because the human experience is so complicated, the nuances of human feelings are overwhelming. And human society moves quickly, much more quickly and adaptably than that of the Or-ta. There have been many changes since I was last on Earth, and I am adrift in them. There is so much more information now, so much speed to human movements. Still, I was unable to find a way to talk to you without surprising you. And I don't know how you feel now because Or-ta are never surprised by the endless possibilities of what can be 'real.' I don't understand what it would be like to not know about the other worlds, to not be able to change shapes, to not know about magic. Even when I take my human form, I don't know what it would be like to believe that this world was essentially the only one."

"Well, in my human form, which is the only one I have, now my life is entirely things that I don't understand, and probably don't believe in."

"What do you believe in?" Ky asked. He realized that, unlike the Earth of his youth, where he had often been mistaken for a demon, or an angel, in this modern world, religion was diverse, and often hidden. When he first started studying Mimi, she hadn't seemed to have a religion, but maybe he was mistaken. "Am I counter to your beliefs?"

"No." She laughed. "No, I didn't mean it like that. Martine is Catholic, but she never talks about it. Dad isn't anything. I was never anything. I never really stopped to think about religion, the 'what's out there' part of religion. In my life that's always seemed more like a political question than a 'real' question. So I didn't worry about it. I meant that I never stopped to wonder if there are beings around like you, who can turn into anything they want."

Ky laughed softly. "Not anything I want, but I appreciate the compliment."

"It's kind of pathetic, but I guess I used to believe that life is short and fun, so enjoy yourself. And then I got sick, and I thought, life is short and brutal, and I don't know what to do."

Ky shook his head sympathetically, but said nothing.

Mimi continued, "There's a lot of talk in the world of chronic illness about your 'new normal.' It's this concept that once you're used to what you've got, it just becomes, your life, your normal life. My neurologist has mentioned it. It came up a few times at the hospital. Even my herbalist mentioned it. I've been resisting it. I didn't want to feel like seizures are normal, or like constant pain is normal. But it does start to become normal. So is encountering beings from other worlds who are magical spies going to become part of my 'new normal' with everything else?"

"Does it feel normal?"

"I think that normal is a very long way away right now," Mimi said. She still felt as though at any moment she could slide back in time to before she knew about Ky, even maybe before she got sick, back to something she could really call normal.

Ky calmly picked up his head and sniffed the air back and forth as though he were looking for a scent but couldn't find it.

"What? What is it?" asked Mimi.

"I don't think it's anything," said Ky. "Maybe something, like an earthquake but far away. Or just a change in the wind. You were saying?"

"I have so many questions I don't even know where to start," Mimi said.

"You don't have to know everything right now."

"Says the dog who appeared as a man in my bedroom last night."

"Fair enough. I will answer the questions that I can without putting you in danger."

"I'm in danger?"

"I'm trying to prevent that."

"But *you* are? You are in danger?"

"Yes, but not here, not today."

A gust of wind swept suddenly through the palms, charging the morning. Mimi wondered for a moment if she'd ever been in danger before. From drugs, she supposed, from being too thin. Those were not quite the same.

"I guess my biggest question is, if you're real...I mean, you *are* real, and so why doesn't everyone know about it? Secrets are almost impossible to keep. I know that. I live what a person might call a 'Hollywood lifestyle.' There are lots of secrets here but, well, they're like open secrets, levels of secrets, the things we know about each other and then the things the public knows."

"And you're currently keeping a secret, one that many people would love to know," said Ky. "But it's different in our case. It's willful disbelief. There was a time when everyone knew about us or about some kinds of magic at least. There are so many more otherworldly beings than shapeshifters, some very powerful, some less so. Now our presence on earth is only represented in your art, movies, stories, songs. There has always been a fight against knowledge, not just of magic, knowledge of all kinds. People tend to shy away from things they can't control. People like rules that put them on top. Even if those rules aren't true, you choose to live as though they are."

"And you don't fit into the rules."

"It may be better that way. We were not necessarily the good guys. We had too much power when magic was

81

assumed and we didn't have to hide as much. Your world is more dependable now. Sure, there are disadvantages, but people like a predictable world. That way people behave predictably."

"Do I behave predictably?"

"You did, but probably not anymore." Ky realized this was true and it worried him a little. What was he doing here confiding in a young human? But Mimi's hands and voice were steady. Maybe she would be fine. Anyway, there was no going back.

"Well, today you have to be on your best, most predictable dog behavior."

"Why's that?"

"Paloma comes tonight."

"Your sister?"

"Sort of. She's Martine's daughter. We grew up together. She might as well be my sister. She's my dad's favorite."

"Because she went to medical school instead of hosting a reality TV series?"

"If you side with her too, I'm going to be mad. A dog is supposed to be a girl's best friend."

"Don't worry. I don't have your same value system."

Paloma drove up that afternoon in her Honda Accord. For a moment Mimi forgot all about Ky and felt only that slight surge of jealousy that she always felt toward Paloma. Mimi's father kept Paloma in modest new cars. It was part of the weird game they played where, despite not being her real father, he parented her the way he wished he could parent Mimi. He had tried to buy Mimi a Honda when she was seventeen and she had gone out and gotten herself a vintage Jaguar, bottle green. It was in the garage. How could he love cars so much and expect that Mimi wouldn't? Mimi insisted on being spoiled. Paloma insisted on being good. But there was no one in the world that Mimi loved the way she loved Paloma. Mimi pressed her face to the slats in the patio fence and watched Paloma kiss Martine hello.

"Come out here!" Mimi shouted. Paloma headed for the patio with her long-legged, loping stride. She opened the gate and opened her arms wide for a hug that Mimi fell into naturally.

"How are you feeling?"

Mimi bit her lip to try not to cry. "Better."

"Verdad?"

"No."

"What do they have you on?"

"No idea, it changes every week."

"So far nothing works?" Paloma asked.

"Some of them make me very sick to my stomach. Is that the same as working?"

"Not what I meant. My mamá said you haven't been out of the house."

"She is not counting the patio, then, and the doctor's office."

"Oh wow!" Paloma's eyes fell on Ky. "Is that the dog? He's beautiful! C'mere boy, c'mere!"

Mimi flushed and looked ashamedly at Ky who, to her surprise, came running over and let himself be scratched behind the ears by Paloma, while enthusiastically wagging his tail. He actually looked like he was enjoying it.

"Oh he's precious! Does he fetch?" Paloma asked.

"No! He's a highly trained service dog. The trainer was very specific. He's at work twenty-four hours a day, seven days a week."

"Do you have a tennis ball? Let's take him to the park."

"You never hear anything I say."

"C'mon Mimi, I know you haven't been out of the house." Paloma started walking back to her car. "I'll drive. How much warning does the dog give you?"

"Ten minutes."

"Okay, well, if you have a seizure I'll just throw my sweater over your head and no one will know it's you. Keep a lookout for paparazzi."

"How long do I have?" Mimi whispered to Ky.

"You're clear until tonight, ten o'clock," he whispered back.

"Okay, we can go," Mimi said aloud. She let herself be dragged into the passenger seat. Ky hopped in the back.

"Mamá, vamos a park!" Paloma shouted toward the house.

Mimi was surprised that she was leaving the house; even with Ky's assurance, she was terrified of going out, terrified of being seen. She thought people would somehow be able to tell that she was different now. Was she strangely pale? She realized that she wasn't wearing makeup.

"Paloma, I'm not wearing makeup!"

"Good, then you can do whatever you want because really no one will recognize you."

"You're awful. I don't wear *that* much makeup."

"You do, but I'm not saying you need it. Look, I'm not wearing makeup either."

"But you're very pretty," Mimi whined.

"I'm rubber, you're glue…" Paloma chanted. They parked and got out of the car by the baseball diamond and strolled along the footpath. Paloma took off her shoes. Mimi's eyes darted around for curious onlookers, but the park seemed quiet. Still, she put her hair up in a knot and tried to rock a casual look. She wondered why. If she wasn't going to do the show or anything else, ever, except pick up a disability check, why did she feel like she needed to look good? It was habit.

"So, no season two of 'Mimi does Europe'?" Paloma held Ky's leash, which made Mimi feel uncomfortable. Ky looked relaxed. He had his head up letting the wind rustle his ears. His nose moved side to side, blithely searching out the air.

"How do you think that would go?" Mimi responded. "Something like, 'Check this out: in her couture bag are six different medications and adult diapers!' No, that's not that much fun. They let me out of the contract. I still have Giselle Parfum, but I don't have another photo shoot for a few months. I'm going to think about whether or not to drop it. I don't know if they'll keep me without 'Mimi

Does Europe,' but they might. They might even like that suddenly I'm so elusive. You know how that kind of thing goes. People think you're working on some amazing project or have some dirty secret, which I guess I kind of do, not a dirty one, but a secret."

"You haven't gone public with your illness."

"And so far no one else has either."

"That's good. Are you going to?"

"Like a big reveal in *Vanity Fair* where I could be everyone's moral compass? Hardly. People would probably think it serves me right. Everyone secretly hates rich people. I'm famous for being spoiled and a flirt."

"And being pretty, sexy, funny."

"That doesn't really make people like you. I think the best I can do is quietly disappear."

"That's a little morose."

"It's a little *true*."

"If it makes you feel any better, everyone hates doctors too. And you know who really hates doctors? Eligible bachelors who are remotely cute! I meet a guy and then he says 'What do you do?' and then I say 'Medical school,' and I immediately see his cute little rear running away."

"Still no sweetheart?"

"No. I think I confuse guys, they're like, 'oh somebody's paying for your medical school? So you're rich? But you're not? But you're Latina? And you don't have big boobs?' I'm very confusing." Paloma moved her bare feet to the grass on the side of the path. "The only thing that makes sense about me is that my mom's a housekeeper."

"Your mom is amazing, the way she has taken care of me."

"She thinks you're her kid."

"I am."

"We're kind of a weird family. Do you remember when I told you that my last name wasn't Parks?" Paloma teased.

"I cried," Mimi remembered.

"My mom thought it was so sweet. I think she seriously considered changing her name for you."

"That would have dashed a lot of hopes since dad used to date a lot."

"I wonder why he doesn't now."

"I don't know, getting older, different priorities."

"Maybe he got tired of skinny, aggressive, blond women in well-tailored suits?" Paloma ventured.

Mimi laughed. "I know I did."

"I feel bad for your dad," said Paloma.

"Because of how my mom burned him and now he'll never find true love?"

"Have you talked to her?"

"No." Mimi's brow wrinkled. "I know I should. I will. I just can't yet."

"Do what's healing for you," said Paloma, "and not anything else!"

"Sage advice."

"I guess it's not easy for anybody," Paloma sighed.

"At least it probably makes my dad happy that the TV series is over. Of course it sucks for him that now he can't put pressure on me to get a real job."

"A real job is totally overrated," Paloma said emphatically.

"Now we really will be riches to rags in three generations," said Mimi.

"What?"

"That's what dad told me about my career, I mean, obviously, before I got sick. Now he only says nice things to me. But before I got sick he told me that most wealthy families go riches to rags in three generations because rich kids are so spoiled they think the money will last forever, they don't manage it well, and they don't get jobs."

"I never thought about it. That's probably true! Like pro football players going bankrupt at forty," Paloma mused. "Maybe not rags; Mamá and I only found riches when we found you, though, so we have a couple more generations to go."

"I don't think you count."

"Ummmm, thank you?"

"Maybe if you become a surgeon, of the plastic variety."

"Those people do a lot of good."

"I know it! I live in LA!"

"Besides, if I become a surgeon, I'm going to go do charitable lifesaving surgeries on orphans who don't have access to stuff like medicine and blankets, so I won't be rich. I have to make up for some of the guilt I feel about how lucky I've been with your dad paying for my medical school. Or I'll just go into dermatology and work two days a week so that I can have a nap and a cup of tea every day, and a nice office with lots of plants and a hot receptionist. That actually seems like a great idea right now. But really, I haven't decided."

"They don't ever let you sleep, do they?"

"Not much; that's part of the whole attractive package."

"I don't feel sorry for you."

"I don't feel sorry for me either. That makes it worse. No, you know what makes it worse? What makes it worse is the medical assistant I'm working with at the hospital. She's twenty. She has two kids, one year apart, two different dads. She has a medical assistant degree, which is a one-year degree, *one* year! It can actually be done in less than that. And I am jealous of her life. She's always happy. She's relaxed. She spends weekends at the beach. She still hasn't managed to divorce Baby Daddy number one. She has a restraining order out against Baby Daddy number two. She has a boyfriend who I'm pretty sure spends most of his time smoking weed in the hospital parking lot. I have spent so much of my life and energy trying to make my life not like her life, but on any given moment of any given day…she's happier than I am! She has two adorable kids. I don't have any kids. She has an ex-husband. I don't even have the beginnings of a first husband. She showed me pictures of herself at her wedding. She was eighteen. She looked great! She loved that dress! She walks around the hospital smiling, smiling and crunching on breath mints, constantly, always minty and always happy."

"Don't fool yourself, Paloma. She's happy because of the breath mints. Sugar makes people happy. I know, because the neurologist has me on a no-candy diet."

"Mimi! I feel betrayed. We promised each other we'd never do the trendiest diet."

"Doctor's orders. Are you saying I shouldn't follow those?"

"No one else does." Paloma looked moody.

"The neurologist said I could have a doughnut once a month."

"That sounds like hard science."

"We're just trying it. The herbalist said I should eat whatever my doctor says, as long as it's food that loves me."

"Wha-wha-what?"

"Food that's been prepared for me with love. It's kind of like what the therapist told me when my eating got really bad, that food isn't the enemy, except that it's more on a cellular level. Food that loves you feels good in the body and is easy to digest."

"That also sounds like hard science."

"In fairness, the herbalist doesn't promise hard science. She also believes there's a vitamin that we get from moonlight that hasn't been discovered yet, like vitamin D from the sun, but this one is from the moon."

"I mean, don't rule it out," Paloma mused. "Does she promise results?"

"From what I hear she gets them, although if you ask her, it really depends on the problem."

"So you can just eat candy all the time as long as someone you like makes it for you?"

"No, because I'm trying to obey them both. So I need mostly sugarless love, except for my monthly doughnut, which, by the way, really loves me."

"But anything my mom makes is fair game."

"True. I wonder if she has a lot of cavities?"

"My mom?"

"No, your medical assistant, because of her breath mints."

"What she has is minty breath, a lot of fun, a steady stream of boyfriends, and two beautiful children. She confessed to me the other day that she's cheating on this boyfriend, which is difficult because he's living with her. She met this other guy online and they meet who knows where, she won't tell me, probably because it's the supply closet. And I can't get a date, not one date!"

"Have you tried picking up guys who are smoking in the parking lot?"

"To be perfectly honest, he's not bad looking."

"If you steal this girl's deadbeat boyfriend that she's cheating on, *that*, and only that, would tempt me to go back to making television."

"I don't even have time to steal her boyfriend. She, on the other hand, just took a vacation to Baja, without her kids. She very cleverly got rid of her exes so that she could give their kids back to them for a week and go to Baja. She has a great tan. And now she says she can't get rid of her boyfriend because he owes her the money from the trip to Baja, so she has to keep him around at least until he pays her back. In case you're wondering, he also has a great tan."

"You have a great tan."

"I'm Latina. But I'm pretty sure my long shifts at the hospital are turning my skin green."

"I wasn't going to say anything but yes, you are turning green. Good thing you started out brown. There are probably products that would help with the green. I could ask my stylist...except I think she thinks I fell off the planet."

"I know how to get a tan. Be like my medical assistant. She works an even forty hours a week. She has a healthy glow."

"Oh c'mon, raising two kids on your own and working full-time can't be easy. She can't always be happy."

"She is. She is always happy and she is always minty. And she has so many problems!" Paloma gestured wide to encompass the span of problems.

"Everyone has problems. I mean, I guess I didn't really used to, but I thought I did. Really, Paloma who's going to marry me? Who's going to have two beautiful kids with me? Who am I going to two-time?" Mimi was joking, but the thought brought tears to her eyes anyway. She blinked them away.

"I think you're still super cute, Mimi. I'm sure the whole world still thinks you're super cute. Probably anyone would let you...did you just say 'two-time?' What decade is this? Have you been watching too many old movies again? I believe the correct way to say this is that anyone would let you cheat on them, although now that I say that, it's probably not true. But it would end up on the cover of a magazine, lucky you. Anyway, let's just assume that anyone would let you cheat on them."

"Because they don't know what I'm going through. They don't know how this body aches. They don't know that the tips of my fingers hurt. They don't know that I feel like I'm a million years old." She looked at Ky and suddenly wondered how old he was. Could he be a million years old? What was happening on planet Earth a million years ago? Were there dogs? She was embarrassed that she had no idea. But anyway, he wouldn't have had to be here, on this planet. He wouldn't have had to be a dog. The thought was overwhelming. She would ask.

The path continued down a gentle slope; the dog park opened up on their left. Mimi had never really noticed this part of the park. Even when she was petitioning her father for a pocketbook dog she hadn't thought of herself as going to the dog park. It looked very pleasant, though. Happy dog owners threw frisbees and tennis balls. All sizes and shapes of well-groomed dogs ran around barking joyfully. There was no fence, but trees bounded the wide-open expanse. Mimi gave Ky a confused look. Even though his face didn't change, she could have sworn that he smiled at her.

Paloma squealed, "Ooh, can we let him off the leash?"

"Did I explain to you that he's a highly trained professional? He's like a dog ninja; he's always working. All of his attention is always on me. He probably doesn't even want to play."

"Do you even know what a ninja is?" Paloma reached for Ky's collar and unhooked the leash.

"He probably won't even go anywhere," Mimi said authoritatively.

"Go play, buddy!" Paloma said cheerfully.

Ky looked at Mimi; for a moment she was caught in the depth of his eyes. "Well, go if you want to," she said.

Ky took off like a shot, with a long light stride where he seemed to barely touch the ground, flying deftly over the grass. He circled some other dogs and their owners. He leapt up and caught an errant frisbee and started a game of keep-away with two other dogs, darting back and forth in the late afternoon sunlight.

"Look at that! You got the best dog. He *is* kind of a ninja," said Paloma admiringly.

Mimi felt a swell of pride as she watched him run. He was a big animal and yet light somehow, and agile. Going for the frisbee his jump was perfect, the landing soft and effortless. For a moment her heart soared with him, with the jump, then she thought about her own aching body and felt a sense of plummeting disappointment.

"I am so jealous of healthy people," she said quietly. "I used to wish that I had bigger muscles and higher cheekbones. I had no idea what I could lose. Look at these people," she gestured to the frisbee thrower and another lady calmly walking a dog on a leash. "They wish they could lose five pounds or grow a nice mustache. They aren't going to have a seizure after dinner. Do you think it would be weird if I went up to them and said, 'don't bother losing five pounds! Just enjoy your after dinner drink! Enjoy your consciousness! Enjoy that you don't have to be near a change of clothes all the time!' I used to think that boys break your heart, but nothing breaks your heart like being sick. I mean, it's my own body, my own brain, for God's sake! Why can't I stop it? Why can't I fix it?"

Paloma wrapped her arms around Mimi.

The next morning Paloma left, hesitating at the door. "You know I love you, right? Do you need me to quit this stupid med school thing and be your personal cheerer-upper? Because you know your dad only has like a quarter of a million dollars in it so far, so I know he wouldn't be mad."

"Go be a doctor. I'll be okay. I'm even going to Henry's party."

"Really?"

"Yes."

"I don't like that guy," Paloma said bluntly.

"Wow, turns out nobody does."

"What?"

"I mean, that's good to know. I appreciate your honesty."

"He's too old for you."

"That's probably an understatement."

"Also, he's pompous."

"So am I."

"But you're my sister."

"I'm definitely more pompous than he is."

"But I still think you should go. Wear something pretty and have your picture taken." Paloma mimed aiming a camera at Mimi.

"Doesn't happen any other way," replied Mimi.

Mimi walked inside and approached her cell phone with steely resolve. She had barely looked at it since contacting her agent except to send out a few messages that she was busy and wasn't coming out. She pressed Henry's number. How do you talk to a magic dude who may still think he's kind of your boyfriend, on the phone, now that you know he's magic but he doesn't know you know?

"Henry? Yes, well, I've been busy." Pause. "I've missed you too. Looking forward to it!" Pause. "Well, we'll see. I'm just trying to make sure you have a lot of time for me on Saturday. You know, inaccessibility is Hollywood's most valuable currency." Mimi hung up the phone. It was easier than she thought. She looked out the window. Ky had turned into a person and was swimming in the pool. She walked to the edge as he got out.

"Martine is at the store and swimming is more fun as a man," he said. He transformed into a dog and shook, soaking Mimi.

"Hey! No fair!" she cringed and jumped back.

"But drying off is more fun as a dog," he said as he trotted off to lie in the sun.

CHAPTER 5

Eric flipped idly through the channels in, what was for him, a rare moment of repose. He was hoping to find a rerun so that he wouldn't have to think too much. But his attention was suddenly snagged as a large picture of himself, smiling, came up on the screen. He tried not to watch news programs about himself unless it was absolutely necessary, but the words under his picture caught him off guard: "Eric Ellsworth: Hawk or Dove?"

He left the channel up and kicked off his shoes. It was typical talking heads. No one had anything interesting to say, but they said it fast and loud and with exaggerated articulation. He frowned as the hawkish pundit completely obliterated the dove. She wouldn't even let the man get a word in. And not only that, she considered being called a hawk as a high compliment. "In times like these," she said, "hawks are pulling doves out of their fearful hiding places." She sounded like a two-bit radio preacher.

Eric wanted to think of himself as a statesman, someone who made the right decision, not someone who always made the same decision no matter the circumstances. The hawk pundit was framing him as a guy who would declare war on someone who insulted his tie. But it was more than the personal accusation that bothered him. It was that lately, the more he knew about the world, the more pieces he put on the board, the more he thought that hawks get elected, the more hawkish he noticed he became.

The dove talking head had managed to find a picture of Eric in college at a Gulf War peace rally. He was holding a sign. It was retro even at the time. It said "Give Peace a Chance!" His young face was smiling. There were friends in the picture. He remembered all of their names. They would be tickled to be on television. They would probably email or message him. And he would have to write back, "Haha! I know!" or something similar that made it seem like he was really too busy to notice. In the picture, young Eric had a full head of brown hair. Eric recognized a man who had never run for office, who could only cook hot dogs, who had only one suit. There was a man who hadn't met Sarah yet. Now she was a hawk for sure, if only where family was concerned. As Eric looked at the college picture of himself, he narrowed his eyes at the young, cheerful, political activist. He knew those pictures would ultimately have no effect on his campaign, but he honestly disliked young Eric at that moment. What right did that young man have to give him a moral lecture? Try living in the real world, young man.

The graphic disappeared and the hawk talking head went back to talking over everyone in her loud voice. She was talking about Bahrain. If it all went south in the Middle East, what would a hypothetical President Ellsworth do? Exactly what we need him to do! He would show the world that we are the most powerful nation on Earth. He would not be ashamed or surprised to find himself making hard choices for global security. He would stand tall! He would be the man we need in our hour of need!

Eric sighed and changed the channel. He found a rerun of *Seinfeld*, exactly what he had been looking for, but now he couldn't keep his mind on it. The situation in Bahrain was complicated, not least because of the finding of new, rare, offshore mineral deposits. The sea border was tricky. Right now fringe groups were mining illegally and smuggling the stuff out of the country. It was being used to fund terrorist organizations. Anyone, even young peacenik Eric, could justify bringing that dangerous and illegal trade to a halt. But would brute force accomplish that?

Eric hadn't talked directly to Henry, or anyone at Sonintech for that matter, about any kind of policy or vote. They had made no asks. Only, rather jokingly, had the man they called "Boss" at Sonintech ribbed Eric that if he wanted to be elected, he could not be seen on the company jet. But Eric knew when it came down to it where they would stand on the Bahrain issue. Where did he stand? If he wanted to be president, he would stand with them.

CHAPTER 6

Ky disliked the feeling of the cold, industrial tile under his paws. He could understand why some dogs refused to walk on it. Also, this waiting room smelled like human suffering. He was glad when Mimi reappeared from having her blood drawn and they could be finished with the biweekly neurologist appointment. Mimi exited the neurologist's office with Ky right behind her and made a beeline for the car where Dennis stood basking in the LA sun, waiting to open the car door.

"Straight to Terra's?" asked Dennis. "I believe you have a one o'clock?"

"Yes," said Mimi. She was grateful to be headed straight to her herbalist. Her neurology appointment had been discouraging, and she felt as if she needed an influx of positive energy. She saw Ky's leash lying on the seat and realized that she had forgotten it. Dennis didn't seem to notice.

"Leash?" she whispered to Ky as they rolled onto the freeway.

He inclined his head toward her. He had forgotten too. When he was last on Earth, leashes were uncommon. Training with a falconer in seventeenth-century Holland, he had certainly never had one. That was the last time he had spent many days as a dog in the presence of people. But he didn't dislike the leash. With a leash on, it was easy to tell where your person was. She attached it, and let it drop to the seat between them.

Mimi was looking forward to her appointment with Terra, even though she realized that she hadn't done much of her homework. Terra was big on homework. She wasn't interested in patients who were looking for a miracle cure. Terra had asked her to start a meditation practice, a yoga practice, and to take a bunch of herbs. All Mimi had done was take the herbs. But, Mimi considered, it's not every day that you find out your dog is really a magical spy. She had been justifiably distracted. She decided to try a tactic that had worked for her in high school.

"Dennis, would you help me with my homework?" Mimi asked, leaning forward and resting her chin on the back of the passenger seat.

"Miss?"

"You're a spiritual guy, right?"

"Sure," said Dennis cautiously.

"Last time I saw Terra I asked her a question, and she told me to meditate on a story," said Mimi. "I asked her if she thought everything happens for a reason. And she said that there's a famous story in Buddhism where a boy goes looking for his ox that had run away. After he's been searching for a while, a fog settles on the countryside and both the boy and the ox disappear into the fog. Then the boy finds the ox and rides him home."

"I have heard that story," said Dennis. "It is a famous Zen parable. There are many different versions of it and some beautiful art, ink drawings usually, that illustrate it."

"I know. I Googled it," said Mimi.

"What does the internet say about it?" asked Dennis. He sounded genuinely interested, not just polite, for the first time since Mimi had met him.

"It says the mind is an ox because it's stubborn and hard to control and we all have trouble mastering our thoughts. I couldn't find the fog version. The internet has the ox and the boy disappearing into the full moon."

"Hmm." Dennis made a noncommittal sound that made Mimi think that Dennis might know more about this than Google.

"And the internet has the beautiful drawings, including one of an empty circle."

"Yes," said Dennis. "That can be considered several ways, but often as when the boy realizes that there is no separate self. Everything is one, or everything is nothing."

"That just seems like a lot of words," said Mimi. "I'm not sure how knowing that everything is nothing helps with anything."

"It doesn't help to know it. It helps to experience it. That's why it's a parable and not a lecture. If I just say to you, 'Mimi, everything is nothing, there's no separate self,' that has no meaning to you. But if I say the boy and the ox disappear into the fog…."

"Then I'm equally confused, but in a more fun way?"

"Maybe." Dennis smiled.

"So, if you know the story, what does it have to do with my question? And does everything happen for a reason?" asked Mimi.

The car turned out of the sun, and Dennis put his visor up.

"Mimi, this Terra is a spiritual teacher, right?" asked Dennis.

"Yes, well, for me she's an herbalist, but I think she has studied almost everything. She even has a PhD in something. I can't remember what."

"So maybe the story isn't about your question."

"It was what she said when I asked the question."

"Maybe it's a response to asking a question at all."

"What?"

"You asked her a spiritual question, your first. This story, maybe it's just the first story, the first answer to any question. It's not so much an answer as it is a trailhead. She's saying, 'Start here. This is where the answer begins.'"

Mimi took a moment to wonder why she'd never really talked to Dennis before. "I really wanted an answer to my question," she sighed.

"Have you found the ox?" Dennis' voice was deadpan but with the barest hint of teasing.

"Oh, honestly, I think I am the ox," laughed Mimi. "But I don't want to become enlightened. I want to get better."

"I want you to get better too, miss," said Dennis kindly.

They escaped quickly from the freeway traffic into a neighborhood of mixed shops and residences and pulled up to a low building shaded by a banana palm and a lemon tree. Plants, familiar and unfamiliar, were growing every which way around the windowsills and the door.

Terra was outside when they arrived, her graying hair tied up in a cheap bandana. She put down a watering can and smiled broadly as she saw the car approach. Mimi felt herself relax. She jumped out of the car with Ky.

"This is the dog!" exclaimed Terra happily. "Here he is, how handsome!" Mimi flushed red as though she had been caught out on a date.

"Yes, he's…he's really good at what he does."

"I've been thinking about you," said Terra. "I have a couple of ideas for things we can try. Fewer night terrors since our last visit, I hope?"

Mimi had to laugh. "Yes, the nights have been very different since our last visit." Then she realized something that she hadn't thought about. "Actually, I haven't had any night terrors since I got Ky."

"Wow! That's good news. I'm so glad. He's a beautiful dog. He's different looking."

"He is different from other dogs."

"Is he a specific breed? I'm not very familiar with dog breeds."

Mimi looked at Ky as though expecting him to answer the question. She caught the glimmer of a smile in the corner of his eye.

"I don't know," Mimi answered. "I should know; I mean, I am someone who cares about brands and brand loyalty!" She laughed. "I can't believe that I'm telling you I really don't know. I'll ask…the trainers at the Seizure Dog Center."

Terra smiled her big, supportive smile. "I'm so excited to have him here. I've had patients with emotional support dogs before, but never a seizure alert dog. What a special skill." She turned toward Ky. "You have such a special skill, Ky. Thanks for sharing it."

Ky just wagged his tail and returned Terra's green-eyed gaze. For a moment it looked to Mimi as if Terra suspected the truth.

"C'mon in," said Terra.

Mimi stepped across the threshold to the lobby of Terra's small office. Her windows were all stained glass, for privacy, she said, but they gave the place the look of a tiny cathedral. Long oak tables were spread out for mixing teas and powders. It smelled citrusy today.

"We've been putting cloves, ginger, and dried orange peel into tea bags," explained Terra as though she could read Mimi's mind. "I've been studying with a Chinese medicine doctor, and I've been working on teas that help regulate body heat."

"For your reptile patients?" Mimi quipped.

Terra laughed. "A lot of people feel cold all the time. Unless you have an imbalance or weight deficit, there's no reason to feel cold if you live in LA."

"I have a weight deficit and I don't feel cold," said Mimi.

"You have a very sturdy constitution," said Terra. The way she said it put a little spring in Mimi's step.

A cheerful girl sat behind the reception desk and called out, "Hi, Mimi!" as she and Terra walked back to Terra's office. Ky followed behind them and sat at Mimi's feet beneath the high-backed consulting chair.

Terra settled in to her chair and gave Mimi her full attention. "So, how are you?"

It was such a loaded question that Mimi paused for a moment, realizing she had no idea.

"I just came from a neurology appointment."

"And?"

"We've kind of given up. I can't tolerate most of the anti-seizure meds, and they don't work anyway."

Terra made a sympathetic noise in her throat. "How do you feel about that?"

"Depressed. But I can't say 'depressed' in the neurologist's office because they start breaking out the prescription pad again."

Terra laughed softly. "You're a great patient, Mimi. Don't let anyone make you feel like you're not. You're resilient, you're smart, you can reflect on yourself, you genuinely consider your treatment."

"I don't know. The thought of having a seizure makes me want to hide under the bed, except that I'm the one having the seizure even if I'm under the bed. Sometimes I feel like I have PTSD."

"You might."

"But I keep getting blown up. Then afterward I'm fine, kind of. I'm still not used to them, I guess. I mean, they're very frequent. You'd think I'd just feel like, 'Ho hum, another seizure.'"

"I think it takes a long time to get to the stage where you think 'Ho hum, another seizure.' Losing consciousness is always scary, even if you're not hurt afterward."

"It's scary and it's embarrassing. It's *so* embarrassing. But I don't want to take anti-depressants or anti-anxiety drugs because I want to feel how I feel. If I felt better, I'd want to notice. I want to notice the day that I'm not afraid anymore. And if it ever happens, I want to notice the moment when I'm not embarrassed anymore. I think it's coming. Or, at least, I think it's possible. Do you think that's stupid?"

"No, I don't think anything's stupid, particularly your commitment to self-awareness." Terra paused for a moment. "But be available to changing your mind if you need to. We want the best for you, and that can be a combination of approaches. People have very charged feelings about anti-depressants, and the influence of all those cultural feelings can make it hard to make a good decision."

"I know. But for now I'm not doing it. Also, I'm really vain. I know I don't have my weight under control, but I want to gain about fifteen pounds: I don't want to gain a hundred pounds."

"Okay, but please do work a little harder on the fifteen."

"I will," said Mimi. "Ky loves to eat. I think he'll be a good influence."

Ky turned his back toward her and studiously scratched his ear.

"Good." Terra looked at her thoughtfully. "No thoughts of suicide?"

"No."

"How's your yoga and meditation practice?"

"Um, it was going badly, and now it's not happening at all."

Terra laughed. "Should we try to pick something else? There's some good evidence for using yoga for seizures, but maybe tai chi would be equal. I can look it up. We should try to pick something that you'll actually do. It won't help you any if the thing works, and you won't do it."

"Give me another couple of weeks with yoga and meditation. I've just been, well, you know I haven't been busy, but maybe I've been distracted. I thought about the ox and the boy."

"Oh, you did?" Terra looked pleased.

"Well, briefly. I Googled it and then I asked Dennis about it in the car on the way here. I'm the ox, right?"

Terra laughed. "You're lost?"

"I am. I have no idea what the story has to do with my question."

Terra sighed. "Your question was, 'Does everything happen for a reason?'"

"Yes."

"Is life more interesting if it does? Better? Worse?" Terra asked.

"It would be comforting if it did."

"Why?"

"Because if it doesn't, then everything you do could cause a disaster. Like, if I die in a car wreck on the way home. If everything happens for a reason, then it would have happened anyway, but if it doesn't, then it's the decisions I make that did it. I should never have come here."

"So is the boy happy to have found the ox? Or does he just think it was inevitable. 'Ho hum, here's my ox.'" Terra's question was playful.

"So bad things happen for a reason and are inevitable, but good things we have to work for? So therefore we should be happy but never sad? Is the answer really contained in the story?" Mimi asked. "Am I your dumbest client? Does everyone else understand this story?"

"Not all my clients get stories. I'm an herbalist, you know. But you asked me a big question. It requires a complicated answer."

"Dennis said the story is a trailhead."

"Nice image!" said Terra, "How old is Dennis? Is he single?"

Mimi laughed. "I can find out. So is it the first of many stories?"

"Only if you want them."

"I don't know if I want them. But I want my question answered."

Terra gave her a piercing look. "You may want it answered, or you may be testing me. I know it's not the deepest question of your heart."

The room felt suddenly quiet and close. A veil of seriousness dropped over their conversation.

"No?" replied Mimi hesitantly.

"No," said Terra. "But that's okay, you don't have to ask me that question if you don't want to."

Mimi was puzzled. What did Terra think was her deepest question? She didn't respond right away. Then she gave a soft, "Oh." She averted her gaze from Terra's sharp eyes. "I know what you mean. I know what the real question is."

Terra nodded a slow, supportive nod.

"It's– will I ever get better?"

Terra nodded again.

"…and, am I being punished, is my illness a punishment," Mimi finished flatly.

"Yes, those are your questions."

"I know the punishment one is stupid." Mimi knit her hands together in embarrassment. "I mean, if illness were a punishment, then good people would never get sick, and that's not true. But I can't help thinking about it anyway."

"It's not stupid. It's natural. It's cultural. We live in a world that seeks to punish wrongdoing. We were all punished as children, so when we feel hurt we assume we're being punished. It would be a logical answer to the

110

question *why*. It may even be a comfortable answer. In many ways we're more afraid to live in a world with no *why* than we are of being punished. But we know that with illness it doesn't make sense because, as you pointed out, good people get sick. Your questions are centuries old. People with and without illnesses like yours have been consumed by those questions: Why me? Did I do something to create this? Can I undo it? And what will happen next?"

"Don't tell me yet what will happen next, if I'm going to get better, if you know," said Mimi. "I couldn't bear to hear no."

"I don't know Mimi, how could I? I'm not a fortune teller," Terra said gently. "Not even your doctors know."

Mimi smiled a weak smile. "Well, I guess I'll just go looking for my ox, then."

Terra's round face was full of sympathy.

"But I have a question about the ox, too," said Mimi.

"What is it?"

"Once I've found it, what will I want if I take that road? Will I still want to get better? I'm afraid to stop wanting…."

"I don't know," said Terra. "I'm still looking for the ox."

They sat in silence for a few moments before Mimi changed the subject.

"I'm going to start going out again, a little, like, socially," said Mimi.

"Great! Is that because of the dog?"

"Yes," Mimi said. It was true, after all.

"That's remarkable. I'm proud of you. But you're not going to tell anyone about your illness?"

"No, I'm going to…well, I guess I'll pretend he's a pet."

"What do you need from me?"

"I don't know, maybe just your approval."

"You have it. I'm also going to add some more things to your powder specifically for the nerve pain. I've been doing some research. What else is there?"

"If I hadn't just given you my anti–anti-anxiety speech, I would ask for some more of what you gave me last time for night terrors."

"The lemon balm?"

"Yes."

"It's so mild. I'm glad it works well for you. I'll give you some of the pills, and if you want, I'll also give you some of the source. How good are you at keeping plants alive?"

"Ummm."

"Just try it. If it doesn't work out, it doesn't work out. Even if you're taking the pills, it's nice to have the plant nearby. It sort of reminds the pills of their roots. Pun intended!" Terra gave a gleeful smile.

Mimi thought about all the houseplants that she and Paloma had killed, houseplants and goldfish. Of course, they had really wanted a dog. "Terra, just out of curiosity, what would you think about someone if they're addicted to peppermints?"

"Are you?"

"No, my sister's medical assistant is. I'm just curious."

"Well peppermints are candies, so that might be what it is. But if it's really the mint in peppermint that she wants? Mint is good for so many things." Terra touched her index fingers absentmindedly to her thumbs. It was her thinking gesture. "I think the most obvious thing about peppermint is that it's life affirming. If you need to believe that we're here for a purpose, that there's a reason to get up in the morning, that the world is a good place, peppermint is helpful. I mean, think about it. It's one of the few things that almost everyone is willing to put in their mouth every night in toothpaste. We put it in candy canes in the middle of winter when we all need an emotional boost." Terra laughed. She met Mimi's eyes, and the sides of her face crinkled up with joy.

"What?" asked Mimi.

"It's also good for if you need courage; for example, if you have a secret."

Mimi couldn't help it; her eyes flitted to Ky, who was lying on the floor peacefully, head stretched out on the carpet.

CHAPTER 7

The day of the gala felt ominous to Mimi despite Ky's assurances. 12:20 a.m., he said, would be her first and only seizure of the night. They would have plenty of time before that, back in the limo by midnight.

"Like Cinderella."

"As normal as you can."

"You try being me and acting normal."

"I'll change all your drinks to water. Drink as much as you like. It won't effect you, but it will likely help you distract Henry."

"You can do that?"

"It is in the nature of the trickster. Can you pretend to be drunk?"

"It is in the nature of the party girl."

They passed the gate and approached Henry's house. It was a large, gothic affair. Mimi had been there many times before, but had never realized what a perfect location it would be to shoot a murder mystery show. The gray gables rose up, forbidding against the night sky. The stonework was pale in the evening light, and cold. The columns that she'd always admired looked creepy to her now; even the fashionable outside lighting looked eerie. Ky had told her that Henry had more powers than he did. What did that mean for his house, his parties? She looked around and wondered what was a trickster's illusion and what was real.

"I can sense him." Ky sniffed out the window. His plan was to hop out of the car before Dennis dropped Mimi off at the red carpet, do reconnaissance around the house, and be back at the car at midnight, simple. If he could get through the night without a direct confrontation, that would be a huge boon.

"Can he sense you?" Mimi struggled to keep the alarm out of her voice.

"I'm hoping he has been a human for too long, and that there's too much going on. What can you tell me about the house? What's the layout? Do you remember anything unusual?"

She pointed to the wing on their left. "That's the library, all three stories," she said. "He's big into books." She gestured at the main part of the house. "The center is where we'll mostly be tonight. There's a great room and a terrace, pool, hot tubs, ordinary stuff. To our right are the bedrooms. Henry's is on the third story." She blushed as she said it.

Ky looked her full in the face. "Drive away at midnight whether I'm back or not."

"Ky, don't–" she started.

"I'm just looking around," said Ky.

Mimi tried to feel his confidence, "Right," she said. "Midnight."

Mimi asked Dennis to stop the car for a moment. She opened the door for Ky, and he faded into the dry, crackly California night. Dennis said nothing. The party music seeped out of the house into the otherwise still night.

They pulled up to the pillared staircase and Mimi took a deep breath. No seizures until midnight, she reminded herself. Here you are in your normal life where you are not sick and where you have no magical companion who maybe wants to kill your boyfriend. Just have a good time. Keep an eye on Henry. She saw Henry standing at the top of the stairs. He was handsome. She thought she saw an inkling of that same not-quite-human eye that was Ky's, something she had never seen before. Well, she thought, once you know something you can't un-know it, whether you want to or not. She walked up the stairs and put on a big smile. Cameras clicked busily. It was a sound she used to love.

"I thought you had disappeared!" he whispered in her ear. She could feel his breath, a little too close.

"I was just busy." She gave him a coy smile.

"Sorry about the cameras. You know how the press loves charity. Together?"

"Sure." She posed with him.

"I'm not interfering too much with your inaccessibility?"

"I too love charity," she said.

116

"Touché." He took her arm. Mimi felt cold; she resisted the urge to pull her arm away, to look desperately behind her for Ky, or to run.

The night was warm and dark. The moon wouldn't be up until after midnight. A few watery stars made a valiant effort against the high smog. From the bushes, Ky watched Henry take Mimi's arm, and for a moment his throat locked with concern. He shouldn't have told her. How could he expect her to have the stamina for a whole night of this artifice? But there was no going back now. He took a crow's shape, glided up and landed on a third-story balcony. From Mimi's description, this should be the wing with the bedrooms, and it should be empty. He took a man's shape and placed his hand on the locked french doors. With a flick of his wrist the lock slid aside, an easy trick for him with a non-magical lock. He opened the door and stepped inside. The whole house stank of deceit. It was amazing that the humans had no idea. They really couldn't smell anything. Be brave, Mimi, he thought.

Henry walked into the house with Mimi, but quickly made his way back to the door to greet more guests. Mimi tried to keep an eye on him. She floated from group to group, making small talk, always facing Henry. She had been out of the party scene for almost a month and it felt both strange and completely natural. All her life Mimi had known how to hold court at a party. It was her skill; she had been so proud of it. Now, in light of her illness, it felt trivial, bordering on bizarre. Why hadn't she gone into neuroscience? She could have helped real people with actual problems. She stood with a beautiful champagne flute in her hand and felt it change instantly to water as it touched her lips. What a horrible trick Ky had played off as an advantage for her. Of course, they didn't know if drinking would affect her seizures and she didn't want to get drunk; better safe than sorry. She saw Henry come back into the room, smiled at him, and then made her way over to him.

Ky walked through the hallways, changing periodically from a dog to a man. On this assignment he had struggled to put all the pieces together. Hal Or-ta, alias Henry Halstead, had been in the human world for too long, was too interested in human affairs, was courting a senator who had a strong chance to run for the United States presidency, may have even created that chance. He was throwing parties for high-powered officials. He had taken a high-profile human girlfriend, Mimi. The Or-ta had abandoned human civilizations two hundred years ago. Except for a few groups of people who had maintained the old ways and traditions, they had limited their contact. Visiting Earth was not prohibited: young Or-ta came occasionally, but briefly, to learn shapes, to see the worlds. But Hal, what was Hal doing? Hal was one of the oldest, and most powerful.

Ky passed from the bedroom wing over the main stairs and the foyer. He could hear the party guests, Mimi's voice, coy, cheerful, and in control with just the slightest edge of discomfort to it. But, he thought, that was to be expected. The question was, would Henry notice? Ky walked toward the library wing, padding as a dog along the soft blue hallway carpet. He disapproved of Hal's décor. It was too ostentatious, he thought, and it was cold. As he approached the second story doors to the library balcony, he heard men's voices from below and a faint smell came to him, familiar, and yet not so. He slipped in through the wooden doors and found himself between high-stacked bookshelves. The interior balcony was narrow; he looked through a low railing at the main floor below, where eight men were sitting on plush leather chairs in a dimly lit circle. Henry was not among them. But there was one, one who might not be human. Ky raised his nose in the air. He still couldn't place the scent. Their conversation wafted up with the clinking of their glasses.

"I think things will really start going our way now that we've hired the right man." The voice was self-congratulatory, relaxed.

"If the prototypes yield any results." A skeptical man, younger, stiff.

"They will." An older, confident man's voice, slightly sinister. "They're perfectly matched, the Boss assured us. They'll be stable."

"I did. And they will be." This voice didn't seem fully human. It was soft, slightly petulant.

"It was bound to happen sooner or later. I just hope we make it work first." The skeptic again.

"The other side has nothing like it. They have to go for quantity, not quality," said the confident man.

"Well, gentlemen, I should be going. Enjoy the festivities." Ky recognized Senator Ellsworth's voice. It carried some false bravado with it. It sounded almost as though he'd like not to hear the conversation.

"Bottoms up, Senator. Tastes good, and it's good for you," said the first voice.

"All he needs it to do is make him a little more influential with the Missus," quipped another voice. They all laughed. Ellsworth's laugh was a little too loud. He sounded nervous. In what company does a man who was almost certain to be elected president feel out of his league, wondered Ky.

They drank their toast then filed out of the library, shaking hands, giving the forced casual goodbyes of those very sure of themselves. Ky reminisced for a moment about a time in his youth when he had been on Earth, just for fun in the late eighteenth century, the time of Masonic halls. He had played a good prank on one group of powerful Masons with the transformation of a skull. He had made it look different to each Mason: for one a mastodon, for one a crocodile, for the Grand Master a kitten. The mastodon took up the whole room. They accused each other of blasphemy. They got confused, bumped into something that wasn't there. Ah, the old days when magic was part of daily life. He watched these men leave the library. Senator Ellsworth and another split off from the group; the rest headed toward the sounds of the party in the main hall. Ky flew as a crow down to the first level of the library. It was quiet. The glasses sitting on the table were empty, down to the last drop. Ky transformed back into a dog and stuck his nose into a glass. It seemed to be scotch, but it wasn't quite. What was it?

He closed his eyes to get a better scent. He inhaled deeply as a human shape crept quietly up behind him.

"The Or-ta think I need to be looked after?" Hal had a booming voice.

Ky shifted quickly, instinctively into a man. It had been many, many years since he had seen Hal Or-ta. If Hal could sneak up on Ky like that when Ky had a dog's shape, he was more powerful than Ky had thought, certainly more powerful than he remembered.

"Hello, Hal."

"You were not invited, Ky Or-ta."

"No, but perhaps my presence was required."

"I think I already have everything I need, thank you."

"Not required by you, Hal, but for the innocent people whose path you have put yourself in."

"Trust me, they are not innocent."

"Can I trust that there will be no innocent blood spilled?"

"Tell Ezik Earth is now mine. He didn't want it anyway."

"What's in the glasses Hal? What are you doing to these people?" Their eyes met. Hal was proud. Ky could feel power coming off him in waves. "I promise if it doesn't break the code, I'll leave you alone."

Hal laughed. "You love your code so much. Have you forgotten whose handiwork brought it about in the first place? Remarkable, that *you* would be the one to tell me not to break the code."

"I have spent many years living with that wound, Hal; you cannot salt it more than I have done myself."

"Nice to hear you're over it, all *those* innocent people, not to mention Or-ta. I don't believe we've spoken since then. There was this little issue of exile. So tell me, did I hear it correctly? Was it really for human love? You were so swept up in their emotions? Or maybe you did it on purpose, hmmm? A setup, so that you could have your precious code?"

Ky's eyes flashed. "The code was a long time coming. You should have created it before I was even born."

"We certainly should have, all the carnage you caused. Don't worry, I don't have anything planned that even comes close to what you did."

Ky said nothing.

Hal continued, "Tell Ezik I'm not coming home just yet. Actually, tell Ezik I'm not coming home ever." Hal raised his voice. He was like talking thunder. Much of an Or-ta's power was in his voice. Ky hadn't heard an elder speak with such force in a long time. It was like being dropped into icy water. He had to brace himself.

Hal then said, "Tell him I love the irony, seeing you here, as protector of the code. Tell him– actually, don't tell him anything…." Hal moved quickly, sending a blast of wind toward Ky. Ky was accustomed to fighting with wind, but the force of Hal's blast was astonishing. It flung him against the wall and pinned him there. Ky tried in vain to shapeshift out of the hold, becoming the dog, then the crow. He shifted back to his human shape, frowned, looked around him at the size of the room, and then burst into the shape of a minke whale crashing down on the floor, out of Hal's grip. The leather chairs were crushed or bounced away and splintered on the floor. He sprang back up as a man.

"Nice," said Hal patronizingly. "But perhaps not nice enough." He threw a blast from his hands at Ky again, but this time Ky lifted his arms just in time, flinging books off the shelves to create a momentary shield. Taking advantage of Hal's inability to see, Ky sent a blast through the books, knocking Hal onto the floor. Ky followed it with his body, but Hal quickly, easily escaped his grip. Ky had never fought anyone like this before.

Hal flung a wide desk at him, then lamps, glasses. Objects flew toward Ky in a swirl of wind. Ky countered, shielding himself with the carpet. In a burst of strength, Ky pulled the stairs from the balcony and threw them between himself and Hal. Hal flicked them out of the way. Ky was breathing heavily. He changed to his kangaroo shape and jumped up onto the balcony.

"You are young," Hal's voice was cold. "You don't know what you're doing with your code of conduct. The Or-ta have become weak. We were involved in the creation of the earth; why shouldn't we control it?" With a single gesture, he pulled down the railing Ky was perched on. Ky jumped clear, became the crow in midair, and landed on two feet as a man.

"Or-ta were not alone at the time of creation," Ky replied.

"You are too young to remember. I am disappointed that they sent *you* after me." Hal picked up a stack of books and hurled them at Ky. In the air they changed into spears. Ky had never seen someone turn paper to metal so easily. The surprise gave Hal a moment's advantage. Ky jumped away, but too late. As he jumped, one spear lodged fully into his stomach. He fell to the ground. Blood rushed hot through his fingers. Hal approached, pulled a real knife from his pocket, and prepared to make the final blow. Ky made a sudden move; the knife caught him in his already open wound. He gasped from the pain but managed to roll clear, stand, and stumble to the open window. He felt Hal close behind him as he jumped, hurtling to the ground.

Hal cursed. He turned into an owl, alighted on the balcony railing, prepared to dive. Then he hesitated, cursed again, and turned back into a man. He ran back through the library and down the steps to the lawn.

CHAPTER 8

Mimi had been looking out the window since she had stupidly lost track of Henry. How could she? Where was he? And more important, had Ky found what he was looking for? Midnight was fast approaching, and despite what Ky said, she had no intention of leaving without him. She was hoping to see his sleek shape running across the lawn to where the limo was parked; instead she saw Henry, injured—limping maybe?—running. Mimi made a split second decision and ran out the door across the lawn faster than she had ever run before.

Henry reached the ground under the library window and looked around warily, bloody knife still drawn. Ky had the advantage now. Henry didn't know Ky's shapes. If Ky had something small he could be anywhere, and small shapes could be dangerous. Hal himself had a scorpion, a deadly one. He heard rustling and shouting from the party. He walked further into the bushes, every sense on alert, when he heard rushing feet and Mimi's voice calling his name.

Mimi came running up to him, shouting, "Henry! Henry, what are you doing?" She caught up with Henry, letting her eyes glance around as much as she dared: no sign of Ky that she could see. She played her best drunk.

"Henry, what are you doing here? Everyone else is up there!" she gestured erratically toward the noise of the party.

"Why, Mimi! I'm flattered that you came looking for me." Henry cursed under his breath, his eyes casting everywhere as Mimi took his arm; he had no choice, he let the knife fall from his hand.

"C'mon, we're going in the hot tub and then the pool!" She tried to pretend she couldn't see that he was distracted, that his eyes were smoldering, his arms were taut. What would she have thought if she didn't know about him? She glanced sideways at his sweaty, angry, glittering face, his expression of violence. She felt a lump in her throat. A thought ran through her mind on repeat. Please, please don't be dead, Ky. Don't be dead. Then it crossed her mind that maybe Henry could read her thoughts. Think drunk, she thought. What does a drunk person say? What does a drunk person do? What does a drunk person think about? She spoke again in her drunk voice. "And then we're going back in the hot tub…and then back in the POOL!" She pulled at him. "I'll tell you a secret. Ready?"

"I just need another minute here," Henry said. He knew Ky was wounded. He could smell the blood, yet he saw nothing that looked out of place. Could Ky have flown away already? He had the crow. Henry looked up at the sky. Maybe Ky wasn't as wounded as Henry had thought. The glare from the party made the horizon dark. He didn't have good night vision in this shape, his human shape. He scanned the low bushes. There was no movement.

"What are you doing?" Mimi asked loudly, shaking his elbow. "Were you going to pee in the bushes? I'm going to tell!" She had no idea what she was going to say next. She decided she needed reinforcements and called out to the nearest guests she could see. "Somebody bring Henry a drink! And me too. Quick! He's not having a good time yet, and it's HIS PARTY!" Henry took a last furtive glance around as a caterer approached them with glasses of champagne. He unwillingly took Mimi's hand.

As they walked up to the steps of the house, Ky could hear their voices receding, ten feet, twenty feet, maybe a safe distance away. It didn't matter anyway; he couldn't stay upright anymore. A small tree with sap leaking down its trunk started to fall in the bushes under the library windows. Just before it hit the ground, it turned silently into a wounded man. Ky covered the wound on his side and his hand filled up with blood. His mind was spinning. By instinct, he tried to change again into the crow, but he didn't have the power. He heard Mimi's voice shouting at Henry, something about champagne. His head swam and he lost consciousness.

Mimi dragged Henry up the steps while stepping out of her dress. She grabbed a bottle of champagne off one of the temporary bars that had been set up for the party and pulled him toward the hot tub, where indeed several partygoers were splashing around in various states of undress. She felt certain Ky and Henry had had an encounter. The question was, how had it gone? Was Ky back at the car, or was he lying dead in the bushes? How could she lose Henry and go back for Ky? She poured Henry a glass and tried to smile at him. She climbed up into the hot tub, never letting go of his arm. When the clock ticked five minutes to midnight, she was fully immersed in Henry's hot tub holding a bottle of champagne in her hand. Henry seemed convinced that she was drunk. He had his arm around her waist underwater. Now that she knew what he was, she found his touch terrifying. How strong was an Or-ta? She had no idea. Was he strong enough to snap her in half? He could drown her, not at a party of course, but still. She thought about all the nights she had spent alone with Henry. Ky had said something about keeping her out of danger. She needed an excuse to get out, get Ky and leave. The champagne to water trick was perhaps not delicious but very convenient. She decided to go with a classic. She chugged the bottle.

"I need a refill."

She hopped out of the tub. Soaking wet, barefoot, and in only her lingerie, she made a beeline for the limo. Dennis was there.

"Ready to go home, miss?" he asked. He didn't say anything about her missing dress, lost shoes. She liked him. He was a professional.

She opened the back door. No Ky.

"I'll just be another minute," she said. She tried to sound casual despite how she felt.

She ran back to where she had found Henry. The library balcony created a deeper shadow against the darkness of the night. She heard a soft moan. Ky lay on the ground perfectly still, his hand covering a gaping stomach wound. She saw him and her heart rate skyrocketed. Her whole body started to shake. She had never seen a wound like that. Somehow she had thought that because he was magical, he wouldn't have guts. She whispered a steady stream of curses under her breath. She could see that his breathing was shallow, but he was breathing.

"Ky, Ky, c'mon." Keep it together, Mimi, she thought. She reached down and took his shoulder. "Ky, we've got to go."

"Don't, don't touch my blood," he said. She thought he was delirious.

"What? I'm not afraid of stuff like that."

"No, really, Mimi, really, it's magic, bad magic."

"Okay, I'm getting your other shoulder. Let's go home." She hoisted him up on the less-wounded side, then glanced at the house. From what she could tell, they were not being watched. She half-carried, half-dragged him out of the bushes.

As she walked, her bare foot caught on something and she felt a searing pain. She cursed again and stumbled. Henry's knife turned over as she kicked it, the blade glowing softly in the dark, still soaked with blood.

It sliced a straight line into the bottom of her foot and she bit her lip to keep from screaming. She stumbled.

Where her blood mingled with Ky's, her new wound opened wide. Just as suddenly as it had opened, it sealed itself closed.

The pain in her foot disappeared abruptly. For a moment she felt dizzy, hot; the world came into sharp focus and the colors of the night deepened. She thought she could see past the stars into the far reaches of space. Time itself seemed to emanate from her, where she stood on the lawn. Ky felt light in her arms, almost as though she had superhuman strength. Lifting him was as easy as lifting her own hand. She gasped. Air filled her lungs and she could sense its substance and power.

She shook her head as if to shake off a dream. And then the world snapped back to normal, as though nothing had changed.

She pulled Ky, as fast as she could, toward the waiting car.

Dennis got out of the car as she approached, opened the doors, and ran up to help her.

Mimi started to babble an excuse as to why she was carrying an injured man, but Dennis gave her a quick look and said, "Get in. You didn't touch the blood, did you?"

"No," she said. She looked at her hands; no blood.

Dennis caught Ky in his gloved hands and laid him gently on one of the back seats of the limo. Mimi lay down on the opposite-facing seat. She felt Dennis close the doors and heard the crunching gravel under the car

130

tires as they started to drive away. She pulled a bite stick out of her purse and looked at her watch. Perfect timing, she thought. Her world became static noise, and she lost consciousness.

Mimi woke up in the morning stretched out in the back of the limo, at home, parked in her garage. The windows and sunroof of the limo were blessedly tinted but through the high windows of the garage she could see that the sun was up in the sky, another balmy mid-morning in Los Angeles. Her legs were cramped underneath her. She wiggled her toes to wake them up, but the right leg was painful, protesting the movement. She must have fallen asleep right after her seizure: foolish to fall asleep on her right side, the bad side, she thought. Then the night before came back to her in a sickening rush of memory: Henry's violent eyes, the champagne to water, Ky's wound, Dennis' seeming to know about him, the blood. She turned to look around. Across from her, Ky's head was resting on the seat but he was awake looking at her, Ky the person. His wound was dressed, but his eyes were glassy. She could hear him pause slightly at the top of each painful breath. She smiled at him.

"I thought I used to have some wild nights," Mimi quipped, "but I have never woken up in a limo in just my lingerie with a half-dead guy before."

Ky managed to shake his head slowly. "That leaves a lot of possibilities for who you have woken up in a limo with, and what you were wearing." Ky laughed weakly. He reached for his bandaged side.

"Yes it does." She smiled. "Although it mostly used to be Paloma and me in the limo. I'm not quite as slutty as everyone thinks."

Ky looked at her with thoughtful seriousness. "Thank you," he said. "You came at just the right moment to save my life."

"You are welcome. Where were you? When Henry was looking for you? We were standing in that spot."

"I was a tree. Henry would have taken a while to guess that. I'm sure he doesn't have one. Trees are uncommon. Or-ta don't usually learn plant shapes, you know, because they don't move much." He laughed and winced.

"Good for hiding, though," she said admiringly. "So much for reconnaissance only!"

"Hal has more power than I could have imagined. He must have known as soon as I was in the house."

"But you got away."

"Thanks to you, and Dennis."

"Did Dennis…?"

"Yes, Dennis covered for us. Martine thinks we're upstairs. Now we just have to find a way to get from here to there without being caught."

"That sounds a lot like high school," she giggled. "So Dennis is–?"

"My man."

"So he is a man?"

"Yes, he's a member of a culture that still believes in us. We have dealings with them, you might say. They live in the far north. We call on them when we need help, human help. They choose a different kind of life, more in harmony with ours."

"But he's really a person."

"Yes. Before I decided to confide in you, he was my way in, before you got sick and needed a dog." He looked at her sober face. She was remarkable. She wasn't mad, she wasn't afraid. She wasn't self-conscious. Maybe confiding in her was a good choice after all. "Is it important to you that Dennis be a person?" he asked.

"I guess, since I thought you were a dog and you weren't, and I thought Henry was a person and he isn't, I'm feeling a little gun-shy, like who else really isn't a person and I don't know it?" She looked at him expectantly.

"That's it, well except, it's not quite the same, but…" Ky started.

"Who? Who else?" she insisted.

"Paloma," Ky said with a wry grin.

"What?"

"Although in her case I'm guessing she doesn't know it either. She's mostly human, very mostly, at least seven-eighths, probably."

"What else is she?"

"Something you would call an Amazon? But they weren't people, they were trans-dimensional. They were travelers; they were only here on Earth for a short period of time. No one knows, not even the Or-ta know where they went, and we've never encountered them anywhere else, although you can find their children on different worlds. They actually did a lot of interbreeding despite their cold reputation." A wistful look crossed Ky's face, thinking about the time of the Amazons.

"So then what about Martine?"

"Fully human; the Amazon must be from the other side."

"Paloma didn't know her father. And Martine is very tight-lipped about him. What can she do? I've never seen her do anything. I mean, nothing weird. Does it change her?"

"Not really. She may have a variety of powers but mostly people don't cultivate powers they don't know about. She's probably very strong for a person. If she decided to become a professional fighter, she'd win a lot."

Mimi laughed at the thought of Paloma fighting at all. Although now that she thought about it, Paloma had been stronger than your average kid. "Is that why Paloma can't get a date?"

"I guess it's possible. Although, as she herself has so aptly described, she's stuck between worlds in a completely different way."

"I didn't realize you were listening to that conversation."

"Dogs have good hearing." Ky flinched as he tried to sit up.

Mimi gave him a concerned look. "We should get you some water or stitches or whiskey or a spell or whatever helps you recover."

"Water would be a good start."

Mimi felt surprisingly invigorated for someone who had spent the night passed out in a limo. She guessed that was the beneficial part of not drinking. She pulled out her phone and sent Martine a text asking for doughnuts from the downtown bakery. She told Ky to duck and peered out the windows of the car. A few moments later, Martine came out of the house. She didn't even look at the limo. She got in her car and drove away. Mimi sighed, relieved.

"Can you walk?" she asked Ky.

"What did you tell Martine?"

"She went to get us doughnuts."

"No one in the world is more spoiled than you."

"Possibly; you're getting a plain one. Dogs don't get frosting. You didn't answer my question."

Ky put his feet down on the floor of the car and tried to put some weight on them. "I don't know," he said.

Dennis had been sitting in front of the limo on a small chair, sleeping with his head propped up on the hood. He stirred when Martine came out but didn't get up. Normally, he would have gone home, but he thought he might be needed. When Mimi opened the door, he came around.

"Miss Parks?"

She jumped. "Dennis! You startled me." Mimi wondered for a moment if she should be angry with Dennis. He'd worked for her for months and she had barely noticed him. All that time he wasn't really a driver at all.

"Do you need help?" Dennis asked.

Ky stepped out of the limo with a hand on the door and a hand on Mimi's arm. His feet touched the ground and he sank into a heap.

"Yes," she said.

They each took a shoulder and walked Ky into the house.

"Dennis, I'm a little offended that you didn't tell Dad in the interview that you intended to take advantage of my drinking habits to spy on me," she sniffed.

"I would have, Miss Mimi, but he never asked."

They maneuvered Ky upstairs and laid him down on Mimi's soft duvet.

"Thank you," he murmured.

Mimi looked at him with a sharp, assessing gaze that she thought she might have absorbed from Martine. He looked bad, but he was definitely better than last night.

"The trick is that we can't let Martine see that you're injured," she said to Ky. "She would baby you! But she'd also want an explanation."

"Fortunately I'm a quick healer," said Ky. He changed into his dog shape without even lifting his head. The wound was beginning to knit together but was still obvious, even under his gray fur. "But maybe I'll lie here for a while," he mumbled with his nose buried in the soft duvet.

"If you think he's okay without me," Mimi said to Dennis, "the shower is calling. I need to smell a lot less like chlorine and crazy, supernatural, party, fight stuff." She headed into her bathroom and closed the door. They heard her turn on the shower and start singing a cheerful mélange of pop tunes.

Dennis walked quietly toward the door but Ky raised his head.

136

"Dennis," he said.

"Yes sir?"

"I'll clean up the blood in the limo tonight."

"I can do it for you, sir. I'll be careful."

"It's too dangerous," said Ky.

"Understood," said Dennis. "I'll lock it then and return it to the rental agency tomorrow."

"Thank you."

"Thank *you,* Ky Or-ta, for the caution."

Ky nodded.

Mimi showered quickly, washing out her hair. She leaped out when she heard Martine return with the doughnuts and went downstairs still drying her head with a towel. Martine was talking on the phone with Mimi's father and didn't see Mimi coming.

"Yes, she went…yes, I think she did. She looked beautiful, of course. Well, I think it's the dog, Mr. Parks. That may have been the best thing." Martine was leaning on the counter, tapping a little rhythm with her bare feet on the sand-colored tile. "Yes, I will. You take care of yourself too."

Mimi laughed to herself, went back to the foot of the stairs, and made some noise. Martine looked around.

"When is Dad back?"

"Next week," said Martine cheerfully.

That evening Mimi picked up pizza and sat in the park eating with Ky. Ky thought he could risk being a man so that none of the well-meaning dog owners would interrupt their conversation to tell Mimi not to feed her dog pizza.

"And so I don't look like I'm insane for talking to you," she added.

They sat on the park bench together for a while without talking, and then Mimi said, "Can I ask you something off topic and then we can go back to stopping Henry? This might be a stupid question."

"It might be," Ky acknowledged. "What is it?"

"Are vampires real?"

Ky laughed a big warm belly laugh, "That *is* a stupid question!" His laugh filled the afternoon air.

"Well sorry, I mean…"

"Don't even tell me you don't know the answer to that."

"Sorry, I just thought because you're real…"

"*Of course* vampires are real!" He was still laughing, he wiped a tear from his eye.

"Really?"

"Yes! They're not as common as they used to be, but *real*, yes they're real."

She still couldn't quite tell if he was joking, but she pursued it anyway, "What about dragons?"

"Extinct, well, sort of extinct. Dragons have complicated biology."

"Unicorns?"

He looked at her suddenly very seriously, "Oh, that one I'm not going to tell you."

"What? Why not? You can't do that. If you know and I don't, you have to tell me!"

"No, we don't talk about unicorns. You may find out one day, but I hope you do not." Any trace of a joke had been wiped from his face.

"Why? I'm going to make you tell me."

"How?"

"I'll trick you into it somehow!"

"Well until you do that, I'm definitely not telling." The smile returned to his face, leaving only a trace of sadness behind his eyes. "Anything else you want to know?"

"Everything," she said nonchalantly.

"Hmm, you and me both."

"Oh wait! At the party I was worried about...can Henry read my mind?"

"I would never have revealed myself to you if I thought he could! Communication of that kind, mind to mind, takes practice and willing participants. Sometimes it can happen, though, if..." Ky hesitated, realizing that he should have been more cautious. "You weren't what you might call 'in love' with him, were you? I assumed you weren't."

"I wasn't."

"Then no. He definitely can't read your mind."

Sausage and mushroom pizza was Mimi's favorite. She never ate it, though, because it was so fattening. But her priorities had changed. Ky had said he didn't have a favorite, so a large sausage and mushroom was quickly disappearing between them.

Mimi looked into the pizza box and picked up the last piece, "Spying makes me hungry. Did you find out anything about Henry?"

Ky was quiet for so long that she thought he hadn't heard her. Then he started softly, "Hal has some kind of new power, terrible power, but he won't change, even in a fight. It's very strange. Our power should come from changing, not from staying the same. He sneaked up on me in the library, which he shouldn't have been able to do when I was in my dog shape, and then he destroyed me in our fight. It was hardly a fight at all."

"Obviously," she agreed.

"Thanks."

"Well, it's true."

"Books to spears. It's so much power. It's estranging something from its very essence." He idly picked up the pizza box and transformed it into a small spear.

"What? But you can do it too!" exclaimed Mimi.

"No, feel it," said Ky, "really."

She reached out her hand tentatively to take the sharp end of the spear. She felt cardboard in her hand. "It's still the pizza box."

"Right, think that could put a big hole in your side?"

"So…"

"I can make it look like anything; well, most things. But to make it behave like metal? It has to be metal. As you know, I can change champagne into water easily."

"A cruel trick," sighed Mimi.

"They're hardly different."

"That's not how I feel about them!" Mimi protested.

Ky continued as though he hadn't heard her. "And I can turn the pizza box into a book." The pizza box flapped around for a moment and then lined itself neatly up into hundreds of pages. Mimi found herself looking at a large open dictionary that was floating just above the bench. "Or a paper airplane." The dictionary obediently dissolved into a large tidily folded paper airplane. "Even maybe a tree or something like that." The paper airplane zoomed around their heads and came to rest on the bench. It grew into a small tree, grew large pink flowers that fell to the ground, then collapsed back to being a pizza box. Mimi kicked one of the flowers with the toe of her shoe; it disappeared. "But paper to metal…." She could see him focus his efforts on the box. It started spinning around out of control, changing rapidly into objects she couldn't quite see, until Ky was clearly exhausted and it fell back to being a pizza box again on the bench. "It's unnatural. Unless…maybe, if the books were specific. But not even Ezik has done that."

"Who's Ezik?"

"My boss, very powerful for an Or-ta, although I also used to think that about myself, before last night."

"You got out alive."

"Thanks to you. But that's another thing."

"What?"

"He would have killed me. I saw it in his eyes, in his fighting style. It's not that Or-ta can't kill, or never have, but it's rare."

"So when you fight?"

"You best your opponent; it's possible to win, to capture. We just don't usually fight to the death."

The park was quiet. Golden evening light filtered through the trees. Mimi had been worried about paparazzi, but Ky said he could use his powers to make them, if not invisible, then at least uninteresting.

"Ky, are you immortal? I mean, if you don't get killed."

"Yes."

"And you can't get sick?" Mimi continued.

Ky looked at her face and became aware of her sudden vulnerability and the turn in conversation. "No, we can't get sick," he said gently.

"That must be so different."

"I imagine it is," said Ky. "I haven't ever thought about not being immortal. Although I have been almost killed a few times in my life, including last night. I've never been wounded like that. I've never bled like that."

"That was pretty gross."

"You handled it well. You could be a nurse."

"I couldn't be," said Mimi. "You didn't hear what I was thinking."

"I heard you cursing like a sailor."

"You were conscious enough for that?"

"Yes, I thought it must really be bad to make you curse like that. I didn't know some of those words were still in fashion."

"Somehow I thought, because you're magical, you wouldn't have guts."

"We can be killed in the shape we're in. The human shape is fragile."

"I feel fragile all the time now," she said putting her hands up to her own stomach. "I used to feel like I was immortal, or I behaved as though I was."

"Don't be too hard on yourself."

"Before I got sick I would excuse myself for doing crazy things by thinking, 'Well, I won't live forever!' or 'I won't be young forever!' I feel like I'm just starting to know what that means."

The evening light glittered on the leaves of the trees, the tops of the grass, her eyelashes.

"I have this dream where I die in pieces; first my hands, then my feet and then my knees are sort of crushed," she admitted. "And I can't do anything about it. And I think in the dream—I won't live forever—but it's completely different from the way I used to think it."

"Is the dream because of the pain from your seizures?"

"I guess so. But also I guess because I'm a person, and we die." She rubbed her hands together unconsciously; there was always a nagging ache in her hands from where they clenched tight with her seizures. She had to keep her fingernails short now, but there were still dig marks on her palms. Sometimes they bled. She ran her fingertips over them. "The pain just helps me realize it."

"You'd rather be immortal, I take it?"

"I'm pretty sure that's not an option. I'm just saying, you can't get sick, and you won't die unless someone kills you, which sounds pretty awesome to me right now, and you're going to risk all that to stop Henry. You already have. I know you were in pain last night. I saw you. You could hardly breathe. You're in pain now."

"Yes. I am. I guess I am willing to risk everything to stop Henry."

"And he wants to kill you and he probably can because he has some crazy power you don't understand."

"Well, Or-ta are not monsters. He doesn't necessarily want to kill me. He just doesn't see another way of getting what he wants."

"But you'd still risk it."

"Of course."

"Why?"

"It's the right thing to do, but also," Ky paused, "there does have to be more to life than just enjoying being immortal."

"I will gladly trade you," said Mimi.

"And then what would you do?" asked Ky.

"Everything, maybe nothing. Go swimming, take a nap. New books, movies, and recipes come out all the time. I would not get bored."

Ky and Mimi sat in silence for a moment, each lost in thought. To any passerby they looked just like two friends on a park bench, relaxing in the evening light.

"There's something I can't explain," Ky said. "I keep going over one moment from last night. It's too strange. I know Henry can fly. He must have at least one flying shape. So why didn't he follow me?"

"Follow you?"

"I jumped out the window. He was right on my heels. He could have had me, but he ran down the stairs instead. Why?"

"Well, maybe we'll find out this weekend…when we meet him in New York."

"What?"

"We're invited to meet him in New York this weekend. Okay; by we, I mean me. I bet that you are really not invited." Ky watched her lips curl up in a little smirk as she made herself laugh. She was terrified of her seizures but here she was, facing the most dangerous opponent currently in her world, and laughing. She was remarkable.

"Mimi, I can't let you do that for me."

"That's not your choice."

"You just told me you'd rather go swimming and take a nap!"

"I said if I were you I'd take a nap. Being immortal and not being in pain? Not even an option for me."

"It's too dangerous."

"What did I just explain to you?"

"I've already put you through too much."

"I promised Henry I'd go. He doesn't suspect me. I'm a better actor than you think."

"It's not about your acting. I can't let you…"

"Let me what? Whore myself out? Are you talking about how I lost my dress? Because, you know, I'm a perfume model; so, really, there isn't anyone who hasn't seen me in lingerie. But if you don't want me to help you, maybe you should have thought about staying my dog for a while!"

"I'm sorry. I didn't mean it that way."

She didn't seem offended, just thoughtful. Hers was a different world from the one Ky had visited last time he'd been on Earth, different because women were different.

"I don't think there will be any hot tub at this party, so my dignity should be safe," she said. "Henry's opening a new flagship liquor store, introducing a new, very high-end product line. It will be an extremely exclusive party. I'll go to the early evening opening. You'll figure out what he's up to without getting speared."

"That's our whole plan?"

"Got anything else?"

"You said he's opening a liquor store?"

"Yes, very high-end. I assume that everyone at the opening will be political cronies. It will be small. I lobbied hard for my invite. I think I only got it because I ignored him for so long. Exclusivity can really work in your favor. I should have done more disappearing when I actually cared about my Hollywood career."

"A party that not even you were invited to? That's interesting. Could he be getting power from these people? It doesn't make sense. We can extract power from some things but usually not without destroying them. And people aren't usually magical, especially political. Wait…"

"Wait what?"

"He's surrounded by all these powerful people and he's stealing, or borrowing, or…no, that's it!"

146

"What's it?"

"That's what was in the scotch! It affects the senator the same way, but less so because he's a man." Ky's face was alight with sudden understanding.

"Scotch? Senator?"

"He's not just giving it out. He's drinking it! If we go to New York, I'll need you to do more than just distract Henry."

"You mean more than just distract Henry and save your life?" Mimi gave him a measured look.

Ky returned her gaze. "Yes, possibly much more."

CHAPTER 9

Oskar picked up the phone. It was one of two in this small Canadian town, and it seldom rang. Telepathy eliminated the need for most electronic devices.

The voice on the other end was calm but insistent. It was a voice Oskar had not heard in more than two hundred years, and one that he was not entirely pleased to hear.

"Ky Or-ta," he said quietly. "You have returned."

The silence on the other end of the line was the most poignant apology Oskar had ever received in his long life.

Oskar let the silence hang in the air for a moment. "Yes, of course I will come."

As he listened to Ky, his frown deepened. "I will leave tonight."

Oskar packed quickly, but before he managed to get out the door, a pale, old face appeared at the window, startling him for a moment. A bare hint of the northern lights played behind her on the horizon, making the face appear paler, ghostlier. In other parts of the hemisphere, it was early fall, but here the leaves were already gone from the trees. The first hint of ice creeped out into the water where the stream slowed down under the walking bridge. Still, she wore only a light dress. For Oskar's people, the cold was refreshing. She walked around to the front of the house, came in without knocking. She sat down on a cushion by the fire and stretched out her bare feet. Despite her ancient face, there was little stiffness to her movements.

"How did you know, Gareeta?" Oskar asked.

"Accidental telepathy. You are agitated."

"I was coming to see you."

"I saved you the trip."

"Ezik has asked for our help."

"Then we will give it," she said simply.

"Yes, we have sworn to give it."

"But you have misgivings?"

"I wasn't expecting to hear from Ky."

"Old wounds still smart?"

"I had rather hoped they wouldn't. I mean, I was my great-grandfather then. Shouldn't that take the edge off?"

"I was my grandmother."

"And you have forgiven."

"Is there another reasonable choice?"

"I know what you lost with the code. You lost more than I. And yet for you, forgiveness comes easily."

She smiled. "Not easily, Oskar, but the code would have come with or without Ky. It was the world that changed."

"I know I am wrong." Oskar looked down.

"We are too old for right and wrong."

"I know. It is an honor to be called."

"It might be both an honor and a terrible chore."

"If it were anyone else. If it were Ezik…"

"Let's hope it doesn't come to that."

"You were Ezik's favorite."

"I was. I like to think I still am." She smiled mischievously.

"This isn't a surprise to you, even my mission. You knew Ky was here, that he might need me?"

"I speak with Ezik. Also, Ky has Dennis Oster, and I speak with him. Ezik had me contact Dennis and arrange his cover. He's in LA. Don't feel too sorry for him; Dennis likes the weather. Dennis was a good choice because he was never in France. He was here in the Americas. He didn't know Ky."

"Why didn't you tell me Ky was here?"

"If he needs your help, it's better he ask for it himself. If I asked on his behalf, you might feel compelled to say yes."

"I'm compelled regardless."

"Still, it's better that you heard it from him."

"Ky and Dennis apparently have a television actress with them. And she knows about him and us."

Gareeta looked surprised. "That's a strange choice to make. But in a way it will be convenient for you. You won't have to pretend anything."

"A television actress," he repeated, gritting his teeth slightly.

150

"It concerns you that her work is television?" asked Gareeta.

"It concerns me that we're taking someone into battle who's not even a telepath."

"She could learn."

"By Saturday? He said he trusts her. Does it seem like we've heard that before?" Oskar's voice was on edge.

"Doomed to repetition, you think?"

"I certainly hope not!"

"This woman knows Hal?" asked Gareeta slowly.

"She was dating Hal."

"Oh, my! Then be kind to her, Oskar. She's already been through a lot," said Gareeta.

"Of course I'll be kind," Oskar said. "But between Hal and Ky, will *kindness* be enough?"

"Ky was never the enemy, Oskar," Gareeta admonished.

"No."

"Ky was young. They can't control how much power they are born with any more than we can."

Oskar put down his pack and remembered his manners. "Tea, Gareeta?"

"I will, thank you," she said.

He put the kettle over the fire.

"I helped design the codes. Are you not mad at me?" she asked.

"I don't miss you. You are still here," he said pointedly. "And I know the codes were necessary. Things are not always better with magic. Maybe it's not Ky. It's something about being of our people. You acquire the pain of many lifetimes of change, not just one. Still, it's ironic that Ezik assigned Ky to enforce the codes on Earth."

"I'm sure that irony was not lost on either of them. Where are you going?"

"New York."

"Then it can't have to do with the time shifts."

"The what?"

"Time is being broken; not big breaks, but unmistakable."

"Enough to pass through?"

"I don't want to make assumptions yet."

"How have I not noticed?"

"The shifts are coming from far away. They are regular, daily, like a machine. But they are not coming from New York. They would be louder." She looked to the south.

"Shall I ask Ky when I see him?"

"Yes, although he hasn't been spending much time in his human form. He may not have noticed. Other shapes aren't as aware of time."

Oskar poured the tea. The rich, grassy aroma filled the small room. She was beautiful. In his great-grandfather's time, she had been taller. She had died young. He remembered the pain of the loss; she hadn't yet passed down all her memories to her daughter. But her daughter's daughter, this physical woman, systematically collected them. She was a powerful woman with a powerful mind. She was the only one of them who still spoke with the Or-ta regularly.

"It was strange to speak with Ky on the phone," Oskar said.

"He probably thought uninvited telepathy would be rude, after all this time."

"I meant that it was strange to speak with him at all. Yes, you're right. To call on the phone was polite."

"You loved him once."

"Who doesn't love a baby?"

"You'll be happy to see him. I know you. You have forgiveness in you."

"The mission is first."

Something about his tone made her look at him keenly. "And it is dangerous?" she asked.

"Yes."

"Very?"

"Yes."

"Then may you succeed to see Ky Or-ta again."

"May I succeed to see you again."

"That as well."

"May I succeed," he said softly. "That will be enough."

Gareeta sipped her tea and watched him walk out the door. Then she rearranged the cushion underneath her so that she could sit in proper meditation. She didn't mind sitting at Oskar's house. All houses were the same to her, especially here in her village, where she'd had a hand in the building of every one. Her braid ran in a smooth channel down her back. The heat from the fire brushed and warmed the sides of her face. The noises of the world became loud in her mind: the crackle of the fire, the sound of Oskar driving away, the movement of wind through dry leaves. She opened a door in her mind and sat by it, steady but unexpectant. Ezik had not been at the door for months now, not since he had wanted her to arrange to send Dennis to California. Her breathing was long and slow. In her mind she opened the door again. There was nothing there. She was not disappointed. She had years, many watchful years behind her. And then, there he was, her favorite, her eternity.

"Gareeta."

"Ezik."

"Thank you for asking for me."

"You look strained."

"You look beautiful."

"I see you haven't forgotten the pleasantries of Earth."

"I haven't." His voice was gentle, tender. In his Or-ta shape she could only see him as a faint outline, and that after hundreds of years of practice, but there was something about the way he held himself. He was tired. She took a moment to take him in, his presence, even when he was troubled, she found peace in him.

"Why have you sent us Ky?"

"You need his protection."

"We need the protection of the council. Why Ky? People don't trust him."

"Not even you?"

"Don't pretend it's simple."

"He only made one mistake."

"But it was the greatest mistake. Am I wrong, or is this a two-part mission?"

"Three."

"Stop Hal, redemption for Ky, and…?"

"Disperse our power. When we are all in the same place, we are vulnerable. Ky needs to be away from Or-ta. He will have a power that is greater than all of ours."

"What's that?"

"Even I don't know everything."

"But you see it."

"I see it in him. He needs to grow up, face his past. Two hundred years is long enough to spend being sorry. He was so adept at learning his shapes. And of course, that was also his downfall. But now he has spent many years in exile. He's ready to come back. We have all made mistakes, but what Ky knows is what it's like to completely lose yourself. There's a wisdom in that. It's a wisdom we will need." Ezik paused for a long time. They sat in the doorway together. To Gareeta there was nothing outside. Even the cozy fire had disappeared. They were mind to mind. Ezik sighed and then continued, "Meanwhile, you're in danger."

"What kind of danger?"

"I can only glimpse it, but I think it's why Hal is there. There's an opportunity now for another Great Forgetting. Hal thinks he can get in at the front, that he can redefine the past and the future with his own cunning, for his own gain. If that happens, I don't know what will happen to Earth or to Or-ta."

"I believe Ky will come through for us."

"The danger is not just from Hal. Hal is only the beginning, and I don't think he's even working alone now. He may just be a pawn. Hal, as you know, is vulnerable to the power of power. Whether Ky succeeds or not, I need you to make a plan."

"A plan for what?"

"A plan to live. You, your daughter, and your granddaughter. You need to save your memories, true memories."

She measured this thought out carefully. "I will make a plan," she said. "What's happening to time, Ezik?"

"I hadn't noticed time changing on Earth. I am far away."

"I know."

"The way you ask makes me worried. Do you want me to guess?"

"You never guess."

"Unfortunately, no. And if I tell you what I fear, then I am only bringing you fear, not information."

"I can wait for the truth."

"It won't be a long wait."

"I will make a plan."

CHAPTER 10

Eric's mind kept drifting to the closet. His mind dug under the boxes and the shoes, and in his daymare came up empty. He wanted to check to make sure that no one had stolen it. But that was crazy. There was no one in the house. He thought about Henry. He counted down the days until their next meeting. He tried to feel casual about it. But when he thought about this coming weekend in New York, the rest of his life paled in comparison. Henry had been clear. This weekend there would be more than enough to go around. This weekend they would each go home with a bottle. Last week when he saw Henry at the gala, Henry had filled up a flask for him. He alone had gotten one, but there was barely a drop left. A bottle, the word was full of promise.

The question was what to tell Sarah. Henry had insisted that she come. Did that mean he wanted her to drink with them? He couldn't mean that. Eric shuddered at the thought of a Sarah who had more power and influence than she already had.

He approached her cautiously. He had waited too long to ask her, and now he was going to have to use all of his charm to get her to go. He steeled himself, walked down the stairs, and found her sitting at her desk in the front room. It was meant to be a dining room, but she used it as her office. She liked all the windows.

"I'm going to New York this weekend," he said carefully.

"Really?" she looked up only momentarily from her work. A charitable mailing was spread out for her either to sign or write short, personalized, and witty notes. Nothing made her more irritable.

"Yes, really, Sarah. I'd like you to come. It's an event with that big donor I was telling you about, Henry Halstead."

"I don't need to go to New York," she said coldly. She continued signing and moving cards across the table, not looking at him.

"I thought you'd want to go."

"And meet your Al Capone? No thank you. I don't want to get caught in the crossfire when the FBI shows up."

"It's not like that. He's just a nice man who has made some very good investments. The reason he wanted our relationship to be secret at first was because he wasn't sure of me."

"Imagine that."

"Sarah, please come."

She detected a note of desperation in his voice that made her all the more happy to deny him.

"Why do you want me there?" she asked. "I'll just be in the way."

"No you won't! I'll be happy to have you. We can go to that French restaurant that you like so much."

"Oh yeah? I'm supposed to believe that we'll do that instead of meeting with rich people the whole time?"

"Scout's honor."

"No."

Eric walked back up the stairs and into his bedroom. He dug around in the shoes and boxes. He hated to do it, but he needed her to go. And if he needed to use that last drop to influence her, so be it. This was not the time to go back and consider fair play. Henry needed her to go. Why did Henry need her to go? No, that was enough. Don't start questioning Henry. He rummaged through the boxes in the bottom of his closet. It was right where he left it. He swished the flask. It made a satisfying sound. A minute later he emerged, smiling.

He touched her shoulder. She looked up, surprised.

"Sarah, rethink it," he said massaging her back. As far as she could remember he had never done that before, not even when they were dating. It felt surprisingly good.

"Okay, maybe," she relented. Was it sweet that he suddenly needed her so desperately? She thought it was perhaps just to keep her quiet about the affair. But of course she wouldn't reveal that. She also had a career.

"Maybe, yes?"

"Give me a day to think about it. And to try to cancel those other events you have me going to."

Eric quickly slinked out of the room.

A text came in that night from Henry. "Is Sarah coming?"

Eric hadn't realized that Henry knew her name. The thought occurred to him that it was a little creepy, but then he laughed it off. He wasn't quite used to being as famous as he was becoming; neither was Sarah. Of course Henry knew her name, everyone did. People knew their faces, his and hers. Everyone knew too that she was the big liability to his campaign. She was strong willed, but she would step up. She had been stepping up. It was growing pains.

He wrote back, "Yes."

Sarah lay in bed that night thinking there was something fishy going on. She kicked at the sheets until they came out from the foot of the bed. She wasn't a bed-maker by nature but she always made the bed now, just in case the press showed up and somehow ended up in her bedroom. She had a feeling Martha Washington was a bed-maker. The press hadn't come into their house yet, but she had so many things she did now just in case the press showed up; why not add one? Even their eating habits had changed. Sarah and Eric could be seen all over the city conspicuously eating pizza with their hands instead of the knife and fork that politicians got in trouble for. The press, once you started thinking about them, became all consuming. Taxes had to be paid for the cleaning lady, registration stickers on the cars had to be updated, cars had to be washed, you couldn't give to beggars, but you also couldn't be caught on camera ignoring them. What a mess, the press.

Had she really been convinced to go to New York? In her mind, she was definitely not going, and then, suddenly, she was going. She wasn't a wishy-washy person, but he *had* been adamant. Lately Eric had seemed so appealing, so charismatic, even to her. She didn't like it. A man you had been married to for many years shouldn't be able to sweet-talk you anymore. It made her doubly irritated because she was so mad at him. She hadn't forgiven him for the affair. One minute she wanted a divorce, and the next minute she didn't. She couldn't get one anyway, and she was restless. She thought about replacing herself with someone else, like in a spy movie. She could hire someone to get plastic surgery to look like her. Then she'd go off to lead a quiet life, and this actress could be first lady of the United States. What a relief. She'd have to tell Eric, but she guessed he'd go along with it. Maybe he'd even thought about doing it himself—dropping her in the river.

He slipped into bed much later, but she was still awake, tossing and turning. "Eric?"

"I thought you were sleeping, honey." He sounded like he had been caught doing something naughty.

"Would you be terribly upset if I hired an actress who looks like me to be your first lady?"

"Don't jinx me, honey."

"You could have sex with her. I wouldn't mind."

"Well, now you're talking," he joked.

"And then I'll go live on a beach somewhere, and I won't say a word about it."

"Hmm. Well, then can we find someone who looks like me too? And I'll come to the beach with you?"

"Then you won't get to have sex with the actress."

"Well, the actor who plays me and the actress who plays you can have sex with each other."

"How does that help us?"

"I don't know. What are you planning for us to do on the beach?"

"Honestly?" She laughed. "Lie around and eat."

It was the first laugh they had shared in a long time. Eric loved her. It was precisely that edge, the one that might lose him the election, that he had fallen in love with. He felt guilt rising up in his throat, and then nausea. He went to the bathroom and turned on the fan, hoping it was loud enough. Then he threw up. This must be what Henry had meant when he said it takes some getting used to. Or maybe there was some rule that he didn't know about against using this power against your wife. Eric didn't want to think about why Henry wanted Sarah in New York.

CHAPTER 11

Mimi tried to explain to Ky that he would need an ID if he wanted to travel on a plane as a man.

"What's that?"

"It's sort of a little card with your name and picture."

"Picture? Show me your ID."

Mimi got out her driver's license and handed it to him.

"I can illusion that," he said. "Just give me something similar to work with."

"They really check it." She fished around in her purse and handed him an old library card.

"Of course."

"They run it through a machine. They look at it, they look at you," she insisted.

"Mmm-hmmm." He looked at the card and felt its plastic edge. "This will do fine."

"Well, we could visit a forger. I know they have them in LA."

"We won't need one."

Mimi was skeptical since they had also only bought one ticket; so, she approached check-in without him. She figured if he was arrested, he could turn himself into a bug or something and escape, but she would be stuck answering odd questions. *Well, you see, officer, he started out as my dog...*

Her check-in went without a hitch, and her plan was to keep walking and let him sort out his own problems, but she couldn't resist watching him as he approached the counter. The airline official looked completely natural, as though Ky was really handing her his ID, although Mimi knew he was not. He walked up to her holding his boarding pass.

"I've never traveled by plane," he said, clearly a little too excited. He looked around the airport cheerfully. "I hate to say it, but for the most part people are doing really well without us. This past century, they have come up with so many interesting things. A plane, very interesting. Even the name is interesting, because of course it planes the air, but it also transcends the normal two-dimensional plane of human existence, the ground. It just goes to show that perseverance is the key. Want to fly, try to fly, want to fly, try to fly, and then, fly!"

"Can't you fly without a plane?"

"Of course. I have a crow, it's one of my shapes."

"Then why are you so impressed?"

"Because you can't. You don't have any other shapes." He said it as though the reason were obvious.

"Should I remind you that we're not having fun, we're flying into a dangerous man's evil plot to destroy the world?"

"Hmmm, and look at all these people just completely willing to get into a plane even though they don't understand the mechanics of flying."

Mimi felt it would be better not to acknowledge that she herself had flown all over the world without the least idea of how a plane flies, except that it helps if it goes really fast. She had been the face of a glorified show about traveling; well, about traveling if you're rich, young, and flamboyant.

Mimi settled into her first-class window seat and took a moment to savor the giggling and pointing that she got as the coach passengers filed by. She loved flying, even if she didn't know how it worked, and maybe a little she still loved being famous. If there had been a camera crew, and no non-human traveling companion, this would be the logical start for another season of "Mimi does Europe." Except, of course, she would be all designer-ed up. And she wouldn't have had to plan the flight for what Ky predicted to be a no-seizure seven-hour period.

"Okay, you caught me," she said as she buckled her seat belt. "I don't know how a plane works."

"But Mimi, your father owns one of the most successful airline consulting businesses in the world!" He sounded genuinely surprised.

"Nice; point out more ways that I'm a failure." She grimaced at him.

"Your father never told you?"

"I wasn't homeschooled! Okay, actually he did tell me, but it doesn't make any sense. Plus he makes software, you know."

"Do you want me to tell you how a plane works?" he asked as the flight attendant demonstrated the seat belt and the oxygen masks that Mimi was always fairly certain were not in the ceiling.

"Maybe; can you do it in ten words or less?" she said idly, turning her attention out the window.

He thought for a moment. "Faster air is thinner than slower air."

She sighed.

"Hmm, no. How about—air over a round surface is thinner than air under a flat surface."

"My father tried to explain it to me once, and I ended up with this visual of air molecules sucking on the top of the wing through tiny drinking straws."

"Add momentum to that and it's not entirely wrong…. Okay, maybe it is."

"Since you can actually fly, you don't even get to talk. You can be a crow. If I could fly, I'd probably know how it works."

"Crows don't fly the way airplanes do, Mimi. Notice how we're not flapping?" He gestured out the window. "And crows aren't actually great flyers. I cultivated that shape because they're interesting thinkers."

"You think in the shape you're in?"

"Partly. Crows think effortlessly in three dimensions; it makes it easier to plan an escape. They're also problem solvers. They are patient. They have some precognition."

"Precognition? Like they can predict the future?"

"Some things about the future; mostly an enemy's next move. They're using evidence for it. It's not magic. There is magical precognition, too. And there's precognition that you get from being old. Even human elders can have that. But what crows have you can think of like chess. They have built-in instincts for chess. That's why you can shoot at crows and sure, they're slow, they're not good flyers, but you never hit one."

"So when you're a crow, you can't get shot?"

"Well, I do things a smart crow would never do."

"And when you're a dog you think dog thoughts?"

"When I'm a dog I think a lot about food."

"And when you're a man?"

"Music, world peace."

The plane rumbled underneath them, speeding up for takeoff.

"Pretty girls?" she couldn't resist.

"Yes, as a man I can recognize a beautiful woman."

"Hey! I just remembered. Was it you on the hospital window?"

"Yes."

"You were stalking me?"

"I like to think I was assessing you."

"For what?"

"I had a few different plans for how to enter Hal's world. You were the best. But I had to make sure you were real. When you fell on the street, it was otherworldly. I was talking to Dennis when you came out of the club. We saw you standing there on the sidewalk.

And then it was as though time stood still, the way your head turned up and you fell. It looked almost as though you were under a spell. I had a moment of doubt that you were even human."

"You saw that?"

"We thought it was just an ordinary night. But then you surprised us both."

"He called the ambulance."

"Calling the ambulance and then staying with you was brave on his part. You had never had a seizure to our knowledge. We weren't sure if Hal had done something to you, if you were a trap for us. But of course, we couldn't leave you there. I flew over you two all the way to the hospital, just in case there was an attack."

"But there wasn't an attack. It was just me."

"It was."

They cleared the first cloud layer and made an elegant curve around LA. People and cars were already dots on the ground. "Ever been to New York?" she asked.

"Not recently, not since it's been called New York."

"That's not really recent."

"No I suppose it's not. It feels recent, though."

"I'm twenty-three. How old are you?" she asked him.

"Older than that." He smiled. "But young for an Or-ta."

"What do you look like when you are Or-ta?"

"What do you mean?"

"Your shape. Can you fly in your real shape? Do you have eyes?"

"Yes and no."

168

"Can you show me? Not now on the plane," she added quickly, "later, at the hotel?"

"It wouldn't be any fun for you. I would be invisible to you."

"So I'll never see the real you?"

"I don't think about how I look as being the real me."

"What about how you think. Is that the real you?" she asked pointedly.

Ky considered for a moment. "Well, what's the real *you*?"

"You might think that's a clever question, but I never think I'm a crow."

"Try it sometime." Ky laughed softly.

"I can't try it."

"I can't not."

"As a man, you can be obnoxious," she huffed.

"That is one of the many skills that's specific to being a person." He smiled. "The dog is less obnoxious. I would turn into the dog for you, but the other passengers would be alarmed."

The early autumn day was high and clear in New York when they arrived. The brightness of the day clashed with Mimi's sense of foreboding. People in the airport seemed cheerful, energized. She had the feeling that they were blissfully unaware of the danger that she knew they were in. Once she and Ky were off the plane, Ky had forgotten his childlike enthusiasm for flying. He was back to his business face: stern brow, watchful eyes. They strode out of the airport together as disguised as they could reasonably get away with, sunglasses, caps. They couldn't risk exposing their relationship to Henry through an inadvertent selfie or celebrity-sighting tweet. They were met by a car with a quiet driver who looked like Dennis but smaller, older, and a little grim. He got out but didn't open the door. The three of them stood on the sidewalk.

"Sir," the man said to Ky, "it is an honor to see you again." Mimi detected a note of—was it sorrow?—in the man's voice. It was an ache, just barely there.

"The honor is mine," Ky said, and then uttered something in a language so beautiful and dramatically different from anything she had ever heard that Mimi caught her breath.

The man responded in kind, and then Ky said in English, "Time?"

"Yes," said the man, looking at Mimi. "She wanted you to know."

"Broken time?"

"You haven't experienced it?"

"I may have. I didn't recognize it for what it was. Your people are more sensitive than I."

"I hadn't noticed it either."

"Let's hope it has nothing to do with Hal. We didn't plan for that kind of surprise." Ky looked at the strange man. "You're injured."

"It was a narrow escape. One of them had some skill."

"But you were successful."

"I was." The man's tone was without drama or humility.

170

"Mimi, this is Oskar," Ky said. The man nodded politely.

"That language?" she said as they got in the back seat.

"It's Or-Ta."

"Oskar is another Or-ta, like you?" They pulled away from the airport.

"No, he maintains the old ways, he's like Dennis. But his people are more formal, more traditional than Dennis. He'll take you to the hotel. You'll have time to check in before your seizure. Your seizure will be at 3:17, and it won't be a long one. Oskar will get you everything you need. I'll meet you at the grand opening." They crossed the Triborough Bridge, the choppy water of the East River cheerfully reflecting the bright autumn sky.

"Where are you going?"

"To find Hal."

"Because of my seizures, I miss all the fun." Mimi pouted.

"I would hardly consider this fun, but if you remember, you were supposed to miss all the fun at the last party. And that did not work out."

"That's a good point!" She brightened up.

"And since you have the most important job tonight–"

"Can you make it so that I'm drinking something besides water this time?"

"Special requests?"

"Strawberry daiquiri?" she said, then in response to Ky's stern look, "Virgin."

"As you wish," he said. "You remember what you need to do."

"I've been going over it and over it in my head."

"Good," he said.

"I wish you would tell me the whole plan."

Oskar pulled over. "Here, Ky Or-Ta," he said.

"Thank you, Oskar. Mimi, knowing the whole plan would not be helpful to you or me if you get caught."

"I just wish I knew, if Henry is so powerful now, how do we expect to beat him?"

"Hal made his own trap." Ky opened the car door and hopped out on the street, pulling his cap low. "Setting it will be the problem."

Mimi felt a slight sense of panic as she watched him walk away. Oskar seemed calm, if still slightly sad. They pulled back out into New York traffic.

They had looked at maps before the trip since Ky hadn't been to New York for more than three hundred years. Mimi had been there recently, but had not been thinking about tactical plans and exit strategies. Henry's boutique liquor store was on Madison Avenue uptown. The hotel was further downtown, an older hotel but a favorite of Mimi's. She liked the old lobbies with the big tiles and gilt doors. Ky liked them because the windows opened, just in case. She checked into their two-room suite. Oskar followed her upstairs, tipped the bellman, and then sat down with the newspaper.

"Do you need anything, Mimi?" he asked.

He was so much like Dennis, Mimi almost felt she was looking at the same person. Almost. But there was something about Oskar; he was quieter, if that was even possible. The corners of Oskar's eyes were weighted with equal parts sadness and kindness. Compared to Oskar, Dennis' reserved manner seemed cheerful.

"Thank you. I think I have everything I need," she said.

Oskar nodded, opened the newspaper, and began to read. Bright autumn sun still poured in the big windows. She closed the door to the bedroom, got out her bite stick, and lay down on the bed.

Mimi was still woozy when she got up from her seizure. Sometimes they left her with a right-side limp, a side effect that made her doctors frown, but not explain. She pounded on her right thigh. "C'mon buddy," she said to her tingly leg. "I need you, game face." She hobbled around the hotel room getting dressed. Her life used to be a lot more glamorous, she thought, but perhaps less interesting. The dress she had chosen for the event was bright red, flamboyant, too much. It was a dress for the old Mimi, which was who she needed to be right now. She thought she could use some of the old Mimi's plucky spirit. This new Mimi—the one who had seizures and was practical and hadn't bothered to shop for matching underwear—this Mimi had some shortcomings.

Oskar was still in the central room of their suite with the newspaper when she appeared, ready for the evening.

"You look very beautiful, Miss Parks." He had the kindly, fatherly tone of an older gentleman.

"Thank you."

"Are you ready?" He had a thick accent. She felt shy in front of him. Here was someone who had grown up speaking the language of magic.

"Sort of," she said. And then, "Oskar, how do you say 'game face' in Or-ta?"

"I do not think it has a direct translation." Oskar was thoughtful. "But you could say something that roughly means 'the only way out is forward.'" He said it in Or-ta. It sounded both hearty and light, beautiful.

"That's true." Mimi laughed.

"For immortals we have a fatalist's sense of time." He smiled.

"You're not immortal, right?"

"My people are not technically immortal. We are people. But we have the memories of our family members, our ancestors, so no and yes. We hold on to our identities through many generations. We live as though we are one with our parents and children. That's why the Or-ta chose us. If you're immortal, it's easier to work with someone who, at least in a sense, is going to be around for a long time."

"You become your parents, like, for real?"

"Yes, and our great-great-great-grandparents as well. We learn their memories; not just what happened, but the texture of their days, their moments, how they felt, what they learned. All people do that to a certain extent. We do it exactly."

"That must be so strange. What if you have a lot of kids? Who gets to be you?"

Oskar smiled. "We don't have a lot of kids."

"So then you also don't have, like, rebellious teenagers?"

"Some of our members leave. They develop personal ambition. We try not to judge."

"Can they come back?"

"Yes, of course. Why not? When you live for so long, you can't hold a grudge." His voice faltered a little at this last thought.

She pondered what he described for a moment in light of her own relationship with her father. She imagined telling him that she wanted to run SkyCut, that she wanted his memories.

"How many years of memories do you have?"

"A thousand. Before that it starts to fade."

"It doesn't seem possible."

"That's why we keep to ourselves."

"How long have you known Ky?"

"I knew Ky when he was born."

"No way!"

"Yes, Ky was born. He was a child, in a sense. He had to create his shapes. I watched him grow up."

"That's hard for me to imagine."

"For me, it's like yesterday. It was spring of the year 1565."

"Wow! Oskar?"

"Yes."

"I'm not immortal in any way. And I'm afraid of what's going to happen today."

He smiled. "Ky Or-ta said you were very brave."

"I'm not."

"But you are. Admitting you are afraid, that is brave."

"I wish I could know that our plan would work."

"I am sympathetic, Miss Parks." Oskar opened the hotel room door for her. "But after a thousand years, I can assure you, the only way out is forward." He said it again, in Or-ta, and the sound of the words gave her courage.

CHAPTER 12

The residents of New York showed their usual cool as a large, gray dog walked off the subway train and started to run down the tunnels. Ky could only hope that he would be in time and that Hal would not have started drinking yet. He had never experienced subway trains before and yet, he thought, underground New York had a smell that he recognized, the smell of optimism and industry, mixed with desperation.

Hal's building had an underground entrance, presumably his choice for importing the unsavory goods that he had shipped there. Ky listened for a moment at the door; nothing, not a sound. Then he took what he knew would be the biggest risk of the night, changed to his smallest shape, and crawled under the door. To his relief, he was alone in the room, a moth amid piles and piles of cash, dollars, euros, yen. The cash too had a particular stink, as pungent as the New York underground. He was glad to be in his moth's shape: as a moth, the smell didn't bother him as much. He flew up to the ceiling where he could get a good vantage point on the room, but as he put his feet down, he felt something soft and unfamiliar. He tried to lift one delicate foot and then another. Nothing. He felt a sudden sickening realization. He was stuck. He couldn't fly away. He changed quickly to a man, but still he was stuck to the ceiling. His eyes flashed around the room, but he couldn't see anything that would help. He couldn't make a whale's shape in here; the space was so small. Ky's eyes came to rest on the door as Hal walked through it, smiling.

"You underestimate me," Hal said cheerfully.

"Probably not," said Ky coolly.

"I didn't underestimate you, though," Hal continued. "You were as easy to snare as I expected; too easy, really. This stuff is my own invention." He gestured at the ceiling. "It's based on their glue of course but I made some refinements. There are so many more interesting polymers now than there were when you were last on Earth, so much more raw material. I've been waiting for you. I didn't imagine you would pass up a trip to New York. I didn't make it a secret."

Ky winced but didn't comment. He couldn't tell what was behind Hal's eyes. If he knew about Mimi, that would be the end of the plan.

Hal continued, "I don't like the small shapes, but I thought you probably would have at least one. I even used to have a seal on the door, but I took it off just to let you in." Hal was smug. Ky hoped he was smug enough to keep talking. "And you crawled in as a moth. Why a moth? No poison, no speed. You make weak choices, Ky Or-ta."

"A moth can have its advantages."

"I can't think of one." Hal made a charade of tapping his temple.

"A moth usually goes unnoticed."

"Well, that didn't work this time, did it?"

Ky didn't answer.

"Do you like my shop?" Hal gestured to a large still that was sitting in the corner amid the cash. It was off, but the piping still dripped brown drops into a bottle close to Ky. "The world has changed since last you were here, Ky. Did you know, people now hire other people to tell them how to be rich? That's *my* job. I'm a financial advisor. And of course, as they say, you have to have money to make money." Hal beamed at the piles of money that surrounded them on the floor. "Everything has changed," he continued. "Look at this paper money! Who would have thought that was a good idea? But it does make such a good, hmmm, it makes such a good *liquid asset*." He chuckled at his own joke. "I like this new century! People are so optimistic. If you remember back to before you ruined everything, we all had to pretend to be divine and then we could get rich. Now they've, shall we say, cut out the middleman? Now you can just pretend to be rich and then get rich!"

"Distilling money, making the power that makes money, clever," Ky said carefully.

"Money is this wonderful thing. It's just an invention, but once it exists, it has inexorable magnetism. You might say it's the human version of magic."

"The still is off," said Ky. "Problems with production?"

"It's a little noisy," replied Henry. "I wanted to be able to hear you come in. I couldn't just leave you stuck to the ceiling forever."

"That was thoughtful," said Ky.

"Not for your sake. I have another guest coming down. The senator is expecting a tour. But now see, you're late, and so your body will be lying around during the tour. It's unfortunate. Or maybe it's not," Hal considered. "The senator is easily intimidated. It's part of why I picked him."

"That's a bit grisly, isn't it?" asked Ky calmly. "Perhaps you've been watching too much of their TV. Tell me, does the senator think that you're human?"

"The senator doesn't think about anything but his future presidency."

"That's encouraging," Ky said dryly.

"I know!" Hal exclaimed. "All that ambition, but for what? He doesn't have any real opinions. You'd think you'd want to be president for a reason, but no, he just wants to be president to be president! It's remarkable."

"That's one way of looking at it. I suppose you have enough opinions that you will be willing to share with him."

"I may have a few pieces of legislation that I'm interested in, a few things in the pipeline, as they say."

"What are you doing with time, Hal?" Ky opened up a telepathic channel to Oskar so that he could hear the response; it was dangerous, but Ky needed him to hear, just in case. He felt Oskar's concern hit him hard in the front of his mind. Oskar had always been a clumsy telepath. Quiet now, thought Ky. Listen only. He can't know you're here.

"Time?" Hal looked at Ky, genuinely confused. And then a smile crept across his face. Ky thought he could have been mistaken, but the smile was one of almost paternal pride. "I'm not doing anything with time. I'm a simple merchant. I only trade in liquor."

Ky tried again. "Don't kid me. You know something about it."

"You're hardly in a position to ask questions." Hal gestured toward the sticky ceiling. He smiled and started to search Ky's eyes. Ky quickly broke the connection to Oskar.

"Not working alone, I see?"

"Saving the world from power-hungry megalomaniacs seems to be a popular cause."

"Ky Or-ta, in case you didn't learn the last time you were in this precious world, it has ONLY power-hungry megalomaniacs. I just choose the best ones and liquor them up."

"Liquor, or distilled power?"

"I go where the market takes me. I may throw you in there when I'm done with you." Henry opened his arms wide in a pantomime of dropping a large heavy object into the still. "You have a couple of talents my drinkers might be interested in, provided you are dead, that is."

"Don't flatter yourself." Ky wriggled helplessly on the ceiling.

"I have other people for that." Hal smiled.

"You've been human for too long, Hal," Ky said quietly.

"You think I should spend more time as a moth?"

"Start with that. I'm guessing it would improve you."

"I'm not that easy to trap, Ky Or-Ta. I may not distill you after all. I am thinking when I have your body, I may send it back to Or-Ta. It will be a warning for Ezik. This is my world now. There won't be any more code, any more fake morality for us to throw at each other."

"Morality's not fake, Hal. Look at what power has done to you. You can't even change. I don't have to trap you; you've built your own trap. Tell me you're not itching to change. I know you have other shapes, and now you're afraid of them—now that you've built up your human to be anything but human. Tell me, what happens to your other shapes now that you're drinking all that money? Are they weak? Sick? Slow? But your human, just the opposite, right? It's too bad that even humans have morals, isn't it. Your minions? They doubt you. They lie awake at night wondering if they are making a deal with the devil."

"I've never met anything as ridiculous as your newfound morality," Hal thundered. "There wasn't a single item in that code that you didn't trespass in your day. You, *YOU,* Ky! You are their devil. You were responsible for Paris!"

Ky let the word "Paris" wash over him with a wave of sorrow and regret as it always did. His stomach turned but his face was stony. "That's how I knew we needed the code."

Hal continued as though he hadn't heard, "And Ezik. Ezik was even worse than you, playing the hero from far away. Want to do humankind a favor? Stay away! At least I'm playing their game. I'm even using their pieces!" He picked up a wad of cash and shook it at Ky. "This stuff? This is their game. This is what they do for fun. If you want to keep this world organized and peaceful, keep morality out of it."

"Your distillery is magic they don't possess."

"One step, one simple step, that's all, just a little push. Give them enough inspiration, they could probably come up with it."

"You agreed to that code. We all did. I paid for my mistakes. I still do."

"But you can't undo them, can you? This is a world full of mortals. In fact, what was your plan for tonight? Everyone but me escapes unharmed? They've already drunk the poison." He gestured to the ceiling where they could hear the faint sounds of partygoers a level above. "You can't get rid of them. I know you won't kill them. You can't stop me now regardless. I have already tarnished the innocent. And what are you going to do about it? Nothing! You have your stupid code."

"The code doesn't keep us from fighting for what's right on Earth."

"Fight? You can't fight me. Neither you nor Ezik nor any of his silly band of righteous idiots is a match for my new strength."

"Which only works if you're human. None of your other shapes would be enhanced by money. That's why you won't change. And that's why you've made powerful friends who can get you the money. And you're so powerful now that you can just lure them right back."

"True, although after tonight, I won't even need to lure them back. Tonight, you might say, the cocktail is special."

Ky looked at the mania behind Hal's eyes and realized it was much worse than he had thought. Right now Mimi was in terrible, terrible danger. Where was she? Had she gotten out of the car?

"Your blood," Ky said thickly. "All these powerful people will drink your blood." How could he warn Mimi to stay away from the party? He tried to open a telepathic channel to Oskar, but the other side was blank.

"You're smart, Ky. Looks like the Or-Ta would have had a bright future with you." Hal smiled at him and nonchalantly gestured upstairs. "They'll think it's their regular dose. They won't even know what has happened to them until it's much too late. They may never know. The senator is not terribly quick on the uptake. His wife is, but, well, sadly for her, she's here too."

"So when Senator Ellsworth runs for president?"

"Let's just say it will be a landslide, my landslide."

"And all these other powerful people?"

"Will get a bigger and bigger slice of the pie."

"And you'll control them. So why pull them back to a feudal system?"

"Easier to manage, it's the corporate structure. You can think of them as middle management."

"More like a bunch of out-of-control lunatics."

"Oh, I don't think they will be out of control."

"It is forbidden!" Ky threw the power of his voice against Hal. He knew at best it would rattle Hal. Hal was too powerful to submit to the command of Ky's voice, but here, on the ceiling, Ky had nothing else. His voice was still strong.

"Forbidden by whom?" Hal shouted. "You already know I'm in charge. None of the Or-ta are close to this powerful!"

Ky realized he was right. And he realized that he had only one chance to live; that chance depended on Mimi not yet having had the scotch.

They heard footsteps on the stairs and a tentative voice in the next room. "Henry?"

"Ah, the senator is here," sighed Hal. He called out, "Just a moment. I'm almost done here, Eric!"

His eyes were glued on Ky. "Much as I'd love to stay and chat, I can't have you ruining my party." He picked up a wad of hundred dollar bills, turned it into a knife, and threw it hard at Ky.

As the knife struck, Ky made a last-ditch effort and changed.

Oskar pulled up in front of the small sign. The street was busy. For a moment Mimi imagined melting into the crowd, hailing a taxi, going to see something on Broadway. What was she doing here in this crazy version of New York? Oskar turned to Mimi and said something in Or-Ta. It sent shivers down her spine. "Good luck," he translated. "I will see you on your return. Oh, and you'll need this." He handed her a package wrapped in brown paper.

"Thanks," she said and slipped it into her oversize couture bag. Purses really are good for something, she thought.

She stepped out onto the sidewalk in front of Henry's shop. The large wooden door was original to the building, but had been refinished. A young man, sharply dressed, opened it for her. The door swung open heavily, like a bank vault. As she stepped across the threshold, she tried to breathe in confidence, like they do in acting classes. She had never needed that for TV, but she needed it now. Breathe in confidence, breathe out confidence. You are the heiress in the red dress, she thought. The party was private, small. She looked around. She was embarrassed to recognize so many politicians. This was not her usual crowd. She walked up to the bar where a tall, beautiful young woman in a tuxedo was pouring snifters of scotch.

"Scotch is all you have?" Mimi asked.

The woman gave her a patronizing smile. "This is a party for a store that sells scotch."

"That's a very good point," said Mimi, and smiled at her own private joke; hers would turn into a shameless daiquiri as it touched her lips. She turned away with her glass, sipped it, and then spit it back into the glass. *That is no daiquiri*, she thought, alarmed. She wasn't sure what the rules were on Ky's drink trick, but she guessed that either meant that there was something very wrong with the scotch or that Ky was somehow…she didn't want to think about that, but her senses went into high alert. She sidled over to the large display window trying to plan her escape. She couldn't see Oskar's car. Should she try to finish their plan, or run for it? She tipped out her glass onto a potted plant and gasped in horror. The ivy seemed to shudder; the leaves became brittle, dried up, curling, crackling in front of her eyes. The stem went soft and drooped. Mimi instinctively stepped in front of it, but she was too late. A well-dressed woman in her fifties came up next to her.

"What did you just do?"

Mimi looked at her, mouth agape. For once she had nothing to say. She tried to stand between the woman and the plant. She looked around her at all the people. They were all drinking, but they didn't seem to be dying just yet.

The woman looked at Mimi's empty glass. "Good God," she said. "That was the scotch?"

"I know what you're thinking." Mimi searched the woman's terrified eyes. "You're not going to die." Mimi tried to sound convincing although she felt like rinsing out her own mouth with soap.

Sarah looked from Mimi to the shrunken ivy. "That couldn't– that's not– was that real?"

"I need maybe ten minutes before you say anything about this, please," Mimi begged.

"What is going on here?" The woman started to raise her voice.

"I know this looks very strange–" Mimi dropped her voice to a whisper.

"It looked very strange long before we got into this situation." Sarah's voice was rolling up in pitch and intensity. "Now it looks downright terrifying."

"I know, I know how it looks, but you'll be okay; I—we—I have a plan for this."

"You have a plan for *that?*" Sarah gestured toward the ivy. "We need help! We need to get out of here! We need to get these people out of here!"

Curious faces were starting to turn toward them. "Look, if you shout right now, it's over for everybody, and I'm not talking about just this everybody." Mimi gestured around her. Her voice was a hiss.

The woman must have believed her because she returned in a whisper, "*I* am leaving. Where's my husband?"

"What?"

"Senator Ellsworth. I'm Sarah Ellsworth." She finished the thought in her head, and I'm the senator's wife. Mimi didn't follow politics, but she knew about the senator's presidential campaign and that his wife was the big liability. She could see why. Sarah Ellsworth's eyebrows were disappearing up her forehead and she was clearly frightened, yet her power and ingenuity were unmistakable. She didn't come across as someone you could placate. If Mimi were older, political, and not in the situation she was in, she could imagine them being friends. Sarah was speaking quickly in a no-nonsense tone of voice.

"I know you're Mimi Parks, I know you're Henry's girlfriend, and I want to know where Henry Halstead got all his money, what we're all doing here, and what's in the scotch." Sarah wasn't much taller than Mimi, but her anger changed her posture so that she was a towering figure.

At that moment, they heard a boom from the basement and the building shook slightly. The guests looked at each other, but quickly shrugged and resumed their conversations. Mimi looked around for the top of the stairs. The bang was Mimi's cue. It meant the plan was still on, she hoped. She saw the top of the banister behind the bar, charmingly decorated with golden party ribbons. The stairs down were unlit. She pulled out the package and stuffed her oversized purse behind the flowerpot.

"Come with me," she said, grabbing Sarah's arm. "But quietly and say nothing, *nothing*."

Ky felt a tearing sensation as his fur ripped out of his skin and he fell to the ground, Hal's knife in his side. The knife turned into a scattered pile of bloody money as it hit the floor. As he fell, Ky created the thunderclap. It was weaker than he intended. He hoped it was enough for Mimi to hear upstairs. Then Ky lay limp.

Hal approached him and stood over him, readying a final blow.

"You're really going to die in your dog shape?"

Ky said nothing; he didn't move.

"Let's just hope this is enough of a message for Ezik." Hal held up another wad of money and changed it slowly, menacingly, into a sword.

As he was about to strike, he heard Mimi's voice in the next room.

"Oh hello, senator!" she laughed loudly. "Oh my goodness! I didn't know the real party was down here!" she squealed. "I was looking for the bathroom."

Hal closed his eyes to try to test his new powers, but they didn't work on Mimi. She must not have had a drink yet. She didn't leave. He would have to make her leave the room the old-fashioned way. Why had he invited a party girl? He was a sucker for beautiful women. Hal looked down.

Ky was still motionless on the floor, making no move to fight.

Hal strode quickly through the narrow basement doorway into the next storage room where Mimi stood next to the senator who was seated on a cardboard shipping box. Mimi cast a quick glance over Henry's shoulder, but she couldn't see behind him.

"Henry! Why are you keeping everybody important down here with you?" She smiled at him. She was holding a pint bottle of scotch in one hand. "Shall we toast your new business venture?"

Henry smiled. There was no reason not to have Mimi here when she took that first sip. Then he could get rid of her if he wanted to, or keep her, or keep her quiet. She wouldn't be as interesting when she was under his control, but there were other women in the world.

She poured her scotch into their glasses.

Sarah Ellsworth watched them from the dark landing at the bottom of the stairs. She and Mimi had come down the stairs together, but Mimi had warned her not to come further into the basement and not to make a sound. Sarah strained her eyes at the scene. Unlike the upstairs, which looked party perfect, nothing had been remodeled down here for many years. The low ceilings were hung with fluorescent lights. Shipping crates and cardboard boxes were scattered around. It was strange for Sarah to see Mimi's face, the face that she recognized from magazines, framed by this damp and ugly basement. Mimi appeared not to notice the surroundings. She was swaying slightly, and smiling, holding a pint bottle and a glass, nothing like the determined woman she had been a moment ago, upstairs. Contrary to popular belief, Mimi was a good actress, thought Sarah. She remembered the dead plant and felt sick. She bit her lip and pressed herself back into the darkness. Henry stood to the side of Mimi in a second narrow doorway, his large frame blocking the light from another storage room behind him. His face looked agitated, flushed. Behind Henry, Sarah caught a glimpse of stacks and stacks of money, and was that blood? Were they about to drink the scotch again? She saw her husband sitting there on a cardboard box, next to Mimi, glass in hand. She felt her fists tightening. She had no idea what this crazy cover girl was up to, but it didn't seem worth the risk.

Mimi raised her glass.

Sarah couldn't contain herself. She pushed off the wall and came charging into the room, her eyes casting violently side to side as though looking for a clue that she had missed. "What the hell is going on here?"

Eric looked up, aghast.

Mimi muttered some nasty curses silently.

Henry closed his eyes.

Sarah's face softened. Her tone changed dramatically, instantly. "I'm glad I finally found you, darling!" she said.

Mimi stared at her in disbelief. She tried to catch Sarah's eye, but Sarah looked back unseeing, vacant.

Eric looked at Henry, "What have you done to her?" he asked.

Henry hoped the senator had already had a drink. "Why don't you pour a glass for your wife?" he said.

"I've got it!" cried Mimi. Could Henry really think she was that ditzy? She hoped so. She poured from her bottle for Sarah.

"To Henry!" Mimi said, and knocked it back.

Henry and Sarah knocked theirs back as well. The senator looked at the scotch hungrily but warily. He drank, his eyes darting back and forth between Henry and his wife. Mimi watched them all. There seemed to be no change. Sarah was still vacantly smiling at Eric. Henry stood tall and arrogant. Mimi had followed the plan, but it must have failed. Henry shifted position slightly, and again she tried to peer around him and the piles of money. Ky must be in there. She tried to think of a way to get to him. Even if he was dead, she couldn't leave him here.

Then the senator made a surprising jerking movement and everyone looked at him. He fell off the cardboard boxes. He started to choke. At first it was silent; he shook, and then the coughing started. Sarah started to choke as well. Tears ran from her eyes as she grabbed at her throat.

"I'm sorry. I'm sorry, Sarah," the senator gasped.

"What, what have you done?" Sarah asked thinly, and then she turned. "Mimi?"

Mimi could only stare back, still holding the neck of the pint bottle. What had she done? Had she killed them?

She turned to Hal. He was confused and then, he was reaching for his own throat. He looked at Mimi too. She knew she couldn't hide her betrayal, and his eyes flashed violence. For a moment she was frozen to the spot. All she could think was, *he's going to kill me before he dies,* but she still couldn't move. She held the bottle tightly. He reached his hand up, and a blast of wind threw her into the wall. The impact knocked the air out of her lungs, her ribs made an alarming cracking sound, her head forced backwards. She dropped the bottle, and it shattered on the floor. Then his hold released; she stumbled but landed on her feet as she watched him fall to the floor. The room was spinning. She had drunk from the same bottle. She couldn't tell for a moment if she was choking or just winded from impact. She struggled to get her breath.

Hal lay on the floor sputtering. Had she poisoned him? How? He saw above him the flash of a red dress as Mimi regained her breath and balance and rushed past him. She jumped over the pile of bloody money.

She got to Ky's side as he was getting off the floor. He was holding another gruesome wound.

"Similar injury to last time, but on the other side," she said, her voice still weak. "Parties are not good for you."

"Is he down?"

"I think so."

"Are you okay?"

"I don't know. Am I?"

"Yes." He touched the side of her face tenderly with his free hand and breathed a sigh of relief. "Yes, you are. Look at you."

She gave a small laugh. "I'll have to take your word for it."

Ky got up, slipping on loose hundred dollar bills strewn about the floor. He stumbled to Hal's side. Mimi followed, but kept a wide distance from Hal, who was clearly still conscious. She knelt by Sarah's limp body, and with a shaking hand, found that Sarah had a pulse, weak but steady.

"I'm so sorry about that," Mimi whispered to her. She checked the senator's pulse. It was the same. He was alive, but out cold.

"What did you put in it?" Hal spluttered.

"Something much tastier than your formula. I believe I'm now in possession of your powers, yes?"

Hal mumbled something inaudible.

"Mimi, would you go upstairs and get rid of the guests."

"Gladly. Are they okay? Can they just go home?"

Ky looked at her thoughtfully. "Where else do you propose they go?"

"The hospital?"

"There's no treatment for this at one of your hospitals. We can only hope they didn't have very much scotch."

"What if they did?"

"There's no treatment for that either."

"Will they die? Get sick?"

"No, not exactly."

"I'll send them home then. What do I do with the scotch?"

"It's more of a hazard than I thought. Don't touch it. I'll have to return to clean up. The power I have over Hal is temporary, so we need to get him safely back to Or-ta. Just make sure you lock the door behind you when the guests leave."

"Done," she said. Mimi climbed back up the narrow stairs. Walking back into the party was like entering a dream. Up here nothing had happened. Politicians were still hobnobbing around. Streamers still hung from the ceiling. She went to the center of the room and waved her arms, which caused her ribs to smart. She lowered them and shouted, "Okay, party's over! Time to go home!" and then for embellishment, "Henry got arrested!" A moment of absolute silence hung over the crowd. They looked at her as though, for a moment, trying to maintain their poise.

"Arrested," she repeated. "Everybody can leave now." She gestured to the young man manning the door, and he opened it with a flourish. There was almost a collective sigh, and then Mimi shooed people out the door. After some chaos, most of the politicians just disappeared. I must have said the magic word when I said "arrested," she thought.

She held the door as the young man and the pretty bartender in the tuxedo looked at her.

"Just leave," Mimi said. "Wait. Out of curiosity, did you drink the scotch?"

"No," said the woman. "We were told we couldn't. It seemed like a big deal. Do you know why?"

Mimi met her big, innocent, slightly haughty brown eyes. "I do." She offered nothing more.

The woman hesitated for a moment and then walked out into the fading light, pulling off her bow tie.

Mimi looked around the room. She pitied Ky the cleanup, but since she wasn't allowed to touch the scotch, she went out and pulled the great heavy door shut behind her. Oskar drove up to where she was standing on the sidewalk before she even had time to look for him or call for him; his dark eyes looked intently at the building as though he could see what was happening inside.

She sat next to him on the edge of the seat. "Drive around the side," she said, "to the basement delivery entrance."

"Did it go well, Miss Parks?" he asked. With his tone of voice, he could have been asking about a tennis match.

"Everyone is still alive."

He nodded his approval. That clearly met Oskar's definition of going well.

As they rounded the corner, Ky was coming up from a door in the sidewalk. He had a glowering Hal in front of him.

"Where are the senator and his wife?" asked Mimi.

"They passed out. They'll sleep it off. I'll return tonight to clean up Henry's blood. Then I'll call the police about the money. Maybe they'll take pity on the senator and get him out quietly. Maybe not. If he's found in a New York basement with a lot of money of unknown origin, I can't imagine that will be good for his career, but it will probably be good for the political process. And anyway, the senator won't suffer the terrible fate he was about to suffer, at least not completely. Some of the damage cannot be undone."

"Should we leave them a note or something?"

"They won't wake up soon, Mimi."

Mimi glanced back worriedly at where Sarah and Eric were unconscious in the basement. Sarah had almost ruined everything, and yet Mimi liked her.

"It's not entirely their fault, you know," she said. "I think they're probably pretty normal people, or they could be."

"I know," said Ky. "Would you like me to get them out without the help of your police?"

"Oh, I don't know," said Mimi. "I don't think, well, he probably shouldn't be president, you know, now, after this."

Hal gave a sinister laugh and said under his breath, "Find me someone who should."

Hal got into the back seat of the car of his own accord.

"Oskar," said Hal, "it's been quite some time."

"Hal Or-ta," said Oskar, and then something in Or-ta that Mimi didn't understand.

"It's okay, I don't blame you," said Henry.

"Likewise," said Oskar, "I do not blame you. The temptations of this world are great."

"Yes they are," said Hal, gazing straight at Mimi. She squirmed in her seat. She didn't like the way he was looking at her, as if he was looking for a weakness and had found one.

"What did you do to Henry?" she asked Ky.

"A trickster forfeits his power to you if you can make him fall into his own trap. It's an old kind of magic, one of the oldest. I think it shows up in some of your fairy tales. It's the equivalent of casting a spell into a mirror. His plan was to control people with the scotch. It was a trick. But instead he drank ours and didn't know it, double-trick, so we have control over him. I have to admit, having Henry's power is giving me a little indigestion." Ky frowned and looked at his hands. "I feel like picking up a skyscraper and throwing it in the river."

Mimi looked at him, alarmed.

"Don't worry, I'm not going to do it."

"But you could?"

"I don't think so. But that was a lot of human power he was consuming. We'll try not to find out."

"Does he have to ride with us?"

"Just back to the hotel."

"What did we drink?" she asked. "I don't understand why it incapacitated everyone but me."

"That was dicey, actually." Ky smiled. "Not everyone can digest a good thing. But I had high hopes for you."

Mimi again looked alarmed.

"It wouldn't have killed you. It could have made you a little queasy. It was a copy of the Magna Carta."

"The what?"

"A thirteenth-century English document; it gave power to the people, the proletariat, back in the day. Arguably, it ended the feudal system and the absolute power of monarchy in England and, by influence, much of the world. You should read some history."

"I didn't know it could be so useful. How did you get the copy here?"

"Oskar took it from his local high school."

"I'll get them another one," said Oskar ruefully. "I needed it quickly."

"So it wasn't a real one?"

"That wouldn't have been necessary. In fact, the high school copy was better, provided any students had ever read it."

"I can't promise that." Oskar cracked a slight smile.

"As soon as I realized what Hal was doing, I realized the solution was so elegant. Hal was distilling money, that and some other ghastly things. But his distillery was condensing the feeling of the item; simple magic, the simplest, really. He was putting in money. Money has so much power for people. It was giving the drinkers a huge rush of power, charisma, influence. But anything could have been distilled in there. Everything has an essence, energy that could be drunk that way. Remember when I was so confused about the books turning into spears? I was only looking at the energy of the matter. Hal was dealing with the energy of the *content* of the books. Presumably he has quite a few books in his library about weapons, violence, fear. Those are the ones he would have used. Or-ta—and people—sense inner energy. Henry just used a little magic to make the energy of the money liquid. I don't know if anyone has ever thought of it before, but it isn't difficult magic, just ingenious."

Mimi looked at Henry. A flicker of a smile crossed his cold expression.

"All we had to do was take something imbued with the opposite of his intention, put it through the still, and the power disappeared: more than disappeared, it backfired. You may have noticed the still was designed for paper, so the Magna Carta was easy to get all the way through the process into a bottle of very different scotch. Oskar came here two days ago, as soon as you told me we were going to New York. He broke into the shop, distilled the document, stole an empty bottle. Then the only trick was to get Hal to drink it too. You did that."

"That's why Oskar was already here, why you asked him if it had gone well."

"Yes."

"What happened, Oskar?"

"Miss?"

"When you got injured, when you stole the bottle?"

Oskar paused for a moment, then said in a matter-of-fact tone, "Hal had to believe that the first attempt on the building was Ky's. I couldn't risk that it be discovered that I had been there. But I needed a few hours alone in the building, which was heavily guarded until Hal arranged to let Ky believe he was breaking in."

"He had to disable three of Hal's guards," said Ky, "without the other ones noticing, and then administer a light sedative so that when they awoke they would think they had fallen asleep."

"One of them was a good fighter," said Oskar calmly. "Not enough training, though."

"With the drug we could count on them not remembering clearly as long as they didn't have any serious injuries, so Oskar had to disable them without really hurting them. No small endeavor."

"And we had to count on them being embarrassed enough that they wouldn't tell the others."

"Which worked."

"Thank goodness for professional pride."

"Then Oskar went to the distilling equipment, distilled the Magna Carta, and gave the bottle to you."

"Wow," said Mimi. "I'm glad I didn't know about that part."

"See," said Ky. "I told you not knowing the plan was for your safety."

"More like for my sanity."

"Oskar hasn't lost a fight in a thousand years," said Ky. Mimi could hear gentle chiding in his voice.

"That's not true," said Oskar. "I lost a fight with Hal seven hundred years ago." He nodded respectfully toward Hal.

"All right. Oskar hasn't lost a fight with another *human* in a thousand years."

"More accurate, unless you count myself."

"I do not count that," said Ky.

"Whoa." Mimi looked at Oskar. "If you become your parents, there's more than one of you alive at once! I didn't even think about that."

"That means I usually have a very able opponent," said Oskar.

"See, he's not always humble." Ky laughed. "But that is the truth. Oskar is the best. That's why I asked for him."

A glance passed between them that Mimi did not understand.

It was almost seven o'clock. The sun had started to sink and make the beautiful autumn day cold. Oskar made his way deftly through the New York evening traffic.

"The Magna Carta," said Mimi, amused. She was still slightly buzzed. "I'll look it up."

"There's a lot of good stuff in that document, but the trap, of course, the trap was that it was the opposite of Hal's intention."

"I was worried about drinking it, but I feel great, kind of good-drunk."

"That's a good sign about your morals." Ky laughed.

"So all those poor people drank Henry's formula."

"We thought it was just money and power. Even though those are not to be trifled with, they do wear off.

We didn't know about the blood," said Ky sadly. "We didn't think he would be so brash."

Henry had been listening to them, not speaking, but now he spoke up, his voice low, menacing. He addressed Mimi. "You were working with him the whole time?"

"Not the whole time," said Mimi. "we met very recently. Plus, you don't get to be mad. I get to be mad. You're the one who was just using me."

Hal smirked. "And what was he doing?" He gestured toward Ky.

Mimi thought for a moment. "Using me for good instead of evil?" She glanced at Ky. He nodded and shrugged. He was amused by her answer.

Hal continued, "You may find that those two things are not as different as you'd like them to be. Ky has not always been a knight in shining armor, you know."

"You're in an awkward position to say that to the lady," said Ky.

"Now you've put the lady in an awkward position, haven't you?" said Henry.

"Well, right now you're harmless, and I hardly think you'll be allowed to leave Or-ta in her lifetime," Ky replied.

"That's not what I'm talking about, Ky."

"Then what are you talking about?"

A twinkle played behind Hal's eyes. "You don't know yet, do you?"

"Know what, Hal?" Ky was stern.

"Oh, I don't think I'm going to tell you. But I'll be very happy when you find out."

"Don't test me, Hal. I am in control of your powers, which maybe you should have thought about before you drank all that money." Ky's voice filled the car. Mimi could almost feel the tires start to rise away from the road. She could see Oskar's eyes squinting in the front seat as he tried to concentrate on driving.

"He's just trying to make me upset," said Mimi. "Did I mention he was a bad boyfriend?"

Ky laughed indulgently. "Okay," he said. His voice returned to its regular tones. "Let's get Hal back to Or-ta, shall we?"

The tall buildings passed by. Hal glowered.

Oskar pulled up in front of the hotel. They got out and took the elevator to the top floor, and then the stairs up the last flight to the flat gravel roof. The sharply angled light of the early evening shone on them.

"Why the roof?" asked Mimi.

"Travel between worlds takes time. It's better to be somewhere private. Mostly, no one is looking up to see if there's something weird going on. Also it's easier the higher up you go. From this world I usually travel as a crow. But Hal can't change right now, so—"

Hal gave Ky a withering look.

"You mean you don't just teleport there?" asked Mimi.

"No, Or-ta can't teleport; what made you think we could? We are much faster than people, especially on our own world, which is nice because then it doesn't matter where we land, and I haven't looked at the stars recently so I'm not sure where the overlaps are."

"Overlaps?"

"It's okay," said Ky reassuringly. "Or-ta isn't close, but it is smaller than Earth. I should be back by midnight."

Before Mimi could get out her next question, Ky took Hal by the forearm and to her surprise they started to disappear, slowly, as if they were fading away. She could see the city skyscrapers behind them more and more clearly. Before they completely faded away, Henry turned his face toward her. She thought he gave her an evil wink.

She shuddered. She was standing on the rooftop alone, gravel under her heels, the darkness starting to drape itself around her and the buildings. Suddenly, and quite irrationally, she felt afraid of the dark. She turned and walked toward the rooftop door; her hand shook a little as she turned the handle. She walked down a flight and then took the elevator down to their suite. She was glad to see that Oskar was there. His face was calm, quiet. She could imagine him living through a thousand years of battles. She felt shaky still in her hands, her legs.

"Miss Parks, do you want me to go out and get pizza? Or Chinese food?" he asked.

Mimi burst out laughing. She hadn't noticed that she was starving, and it seemed so normal to her, pizza or Chinese. "That's a great idea," she said, still laughing. "Which would you rather?"

Oskar thought for a moment. "There is no Chinese food in my small town. I'm partial to Chinese."

"Excellent," she said. "Even the thought of lo mein makes my creepy ex-boyfriend problems melt away."

"Give me twenty minutes." He walked out the door.

Ky returned to the hotel late in the evening. Mimi was waiting for him, sitting by the window wrapped up in her pajamas and the hotel bathrobe, sipping tea. She had taken both a bath and a shower.

"There's cold Chinese food."

"That's a way in which Earth is much better than any of the other worlds. I'm glad I didn't eat on Or-ta," Ky said, picking up a package of chopsticks.

"What did you do with the Ellsworths?"

"I talked to them. They left before the police got there. I let them leave. They seem to have enough problems."

"Eric Ellsworth for president?"

"I doubt it." He paused. "But I wouldn't intervene. I don't like human politics much. Can't you sleep?"

"Not quite yet. I'm so tired. This is chamomile tea. It's supposed to help you sleep. I'm not sure the stuff works, though."

"It probably depends on why you're awake," said Ky.

"You took Henry to Or-Ta?"

"Yes."

"And?"

"He will face judgment, certainly banishment from Earth. I'm sorry he was cruel to you in the car. He can't come back, Mimi, despite his threats." There was only one lamp on in the room and just the bare outline of their faces was reflected in the hotel window. Mimi looked past their reflections into the city night.

206

"I'm not…I don't think I'm afraid. I'm just sort of amped up, keyed up. I wish I could have gone with you."

"To Or-ta?"

"Yes. I would have liked to see Hal placed into custody, the custody of whoever it is that will deal with him; Ezik?"

"The council will meet. Yes, Ezik is on it. He assigned me to Earth. He has taken an interest in Earth lately. All the elder Or-ta have. They seem to think it needs extra protection just now."

"Clearly it did."

"Yes, but I wonder why," said Ky.

"You don't know?"

"I think the Or-ta elders…I think they suspect something, but aren't willing to say it yet."

"Suspect what?"

"I don't know. They've been very secretive. Perhaps that Earth is vulnerable, that we made the wrong choice when we left. I shouldn't be talking to you about this. It's conjecture. There's no use being scared about something that might not be happening."

"I'm not scared, Ky."

"No, you're not, are you? You performed admirably today."

"Today I was scared."

"That's only reasonable."

"But scared of the Earth being vulnerable? That just seems to make sense. It certainly feels vulnerable."

"Did it before you met me?"

"I think so, yes."

They sat in silence together staring out into the cool New York evening. They were high enough up that the people on the streets looked remote, inaccessible. They were floating above day-to-day life.

"What will you do now? Are you–" Mimi suddenly felt on uncertain ground. She hadn't actually thought about the future past tonight. "Will you come back to California?"

"I'll fly back with you, then I need to go meet with an elder in Oskar's village."

"Oskar said he remembers when you were born."

"He probably does." Ky smiled. "I don't."

"Their lives are so strange, that they become their parents."

"For centuries they lived close with us, in harmony with our immortal lives. I can't say I'm sorry to be going up there to that cold country where they live. I have many friends there that I haven't seen in a long time, friends who are now their great-great-grandchildren. I look forward to seeing who they've become."

"I had no idea there were people who lived like that."

"They are quiet about it, for obvious reasons. They don't want to end up the subject of a documentary film. A woman in his village, she has noticed something that I did not. I may have another project sooner than I thought."

Mimi looked out the window and frowned. She didn't want to go back to her life, her life of being sick. She knew she didn't need Ky. She should be thinking about another project of her own. She wasn't ready. She hadn't been ready for anything that had happened yet.

Ky continued, "But before that, I'll come back and close this project with Dennis, and with you, Mimi. You fought hard and, well, you deserve closure, and my deepest regards."

"So I lose my dog and my driver?"

"Dennis might stay with you. I don't know what his plans are. I think he enjoys LA. And when I leave, you can get a real dog, one that helps you stay out of trouble." He tried to sound optimistic, but his voice faltered ever so slightly. He had enjoyed working with Mimi, her intrepid smile, her joy. But he reminded himself that she was a person. She needed to live as one.

CHAPTER 13

When they landed in LA, the smog lay in thin, striated sheets. The plane brushed down through them, one after another, the bars of a prison the city had created for itself. Mimi had flown into LA hundreds of times, but she always looked out the window. Usually, when she flew, she loved the takeoff and landing. Today, though, the landing was oppressive for her. The city looked hot and lazy under all those layers of smog after the energy and excitement of New York. Dennis picked them up just outside the baggage claim. Mimi got in the car and immediately put her face against the air conditioning vent. Ky turned back into a dog in the back of the limo and lay down on the seat with his face on his paws, his gray silky brow wrinkled in thought.

As they pulled up to the Parks's 1970s-style mansion, Mimi tried to see it from Ky's perspective, as though she were revisiting Earth after a few hundred years. LA wasn't even that old. It had been a forest or a swamp or something. She didn't remember. Dennis dropped them off at the front door where broad, clean, white steps came up to the big oak paneled door with its ornate windows.

Martine was beaming at them as they came in. Mimi tried to look cheerful. She knew that Martine would be happy if she thought they had had a good time. She might have to admit to Martine that Henry had been arrested… arrested? That would be her story. But not right now.

"Did you have a good time, querida?"

"It was amazing," said Mimi.

"You're feeling okay?"

Mimi realized that she was limping again. "Yes, I just can't sit comfortably, you know, on a plane like that for so long."

"You didn't, you didn't have a seizure on the plane, did you? I know you were worried about that."

"No," Mimi said, "I didn't." She hadn't been worried about it, but she realized that when Ky left, she would have to be. She would be back to a ten-minute warning if she got a new dog. The thought made her gloomy. She wouldn't be going anywhere for a while.

"I'm glad, honey. Is Ky…is your dog limping too?"

Mimi and Ky looked at each other. Ky showed a bare patch of fur and a scar where he had been sliced open with Hal's knife. Mimi hadn't noticed it in the dark limo. They hadn't thought about what to tell Martine. "He just, well, in New York…" Mimi started. "He was hit by a car."

"Oh no!" Martine rushed over to Ky and grabbed his head and kissed it. He wagged his tail. "Should we take him to the vet?"

"No," said Mimi. "Er, I mean, don't worry, we did, in New York. He's fine. The vet said he's fine. He's just sore."

"He looks sore. Poor thing. He's never been to the big city before."

"Kind of."

"I'll get you a treat, my beautiful Ky." Martine went into the pantry.

Ky walked over to Mimi and stood where his wagging tail could hit her repeatedly in the leg. He whispered, "I'm going to miss Martine."

"You're sure you don't want to stay?" Mimi giggled. "That pantry is full of treats, and I mean full."

"It's not a matter of want," said Ky.

Martine returned with an assortment of biscuits and some beef jerky. "Come here, my beautiful injured boy," she said lovingly. Ky walked over and let himself be petted and treated.

"Shameless," Mimi muttered under her breath.

They went to bed that night under the cover of an orange city haze. Mimi tried not to think of the blankness of the days ahead, of her mid-week appointment with the neurologist that would likely go nowhere.

Ky knew they should debrief. But they'd have time for that tomorrow. For now he just lay next to her on the duvet, as a dog, as they met. She scratched him behind the ears.

"You like that, really?" she said. "Now that I know you're a hero sent from another world to do battle with evil forces, I feel silly scratching you behind the ears."

212

"A dog is a dog," said Ky. "And to be scratched behind the ears is the most perfect feeling there is."

In the morning they came down to breakfast. Martine was cheerful. She had made huge quantities of waffles. Mimi tried to not to act like it was her last day with Ky. Her limp was still there. She lingered around the breakfast table and then finally got up her resolve.

"I'm going to take a walk to the park," Mimi said. They had planned their story for Martine and Mimi's father. Ky would "run away" from the park. "I need to exercise this bad leg."

Martine looked surprised but pleased. "Of course! Good idea. Want me to come?"

"No that's all right. I'll just, I'll just take Ky." It hurt her heart to say it, knowing it would be the last time.

"Okay, but don't let him play too hard. He had a tough trip!"

"I won't," said Mimi. "I know he did."

They left the house in silence. Mimi walked behind Ky. She could see his limp. She could hardly believe that two days ago Ky had almost been killed, and here they were, on a walk to the park, leash in hand. As they rounded the corner away from the house they came under the cover of a stand of pines. Ky looked around to make sure no one was watching and then turned in to a man. The leash fell to the ground. Mimi didn't bother to pick it up. She wouldn't need it. Ky's change was graceful, but as a man, his gait was still stiff. They walked in silence together for a while, both nursing their injuries.

"We're in bad shape," said Mimi.

"Better than I expected, at least for me," said Ky. His shirt rubbed where his side was sore.

"Ky, what happens with the blood?"

"Or-ta blood is forbidden."

"Because it lets you control someone? I thought you could do that anyway."

"We can create illusions; that's not the same as control. With our blood we can control people without them even knowing, large groups, armies. There was a time when we targeted powerful people, arranged world events, like Hal was trying to do, back in the early days when Or-ta were more involved. We thought it was okay to control people because we could. But we couldn't control ourselves. It was a shameful time. Many of us were like Henry, taking control wherever we could."

"So you have to be really careful, I mean, with your blood."

"We do. Or-ta are not commonly injured, though."

"You get injured all the time."

"We faced the most powerful enemy an Or-ta has faced in many years," he said with a shrug.

"And won!" said Mimi.

Ky smiled. "And won."

"So it's in your code of laws not to use your blood anymore?"

"Well, there have always been taboos on the blood. Since anyone can remember, it has been forbidden to use

214

it for seduction or to force a suicide. But controlling armies, politicians? That was fair game until the code. Of course, the world was different then. There wasn't the same kind of global power. There were empires, though."

"Did you ever control an empire?"

"No, I'm too young."

"Me too."

"Well, really, you have a certain kind of empire, something you now call a 'brand.'"

She laughed. "My brand? That's over. Even if I could do it with my illness, I don't want to. I don't know how I would start doing something else, though. I'm so famous for being what my father would call a 'ditz.' We humans should have a code like your code, except ours would be against doing stupid things when you're young."

"I think you do. I just think your young don't pay attention to it."

"Would it be better to be like Oskar? Just become your parents?"

"That also comes at a price."

"It might have been better for me. My 'brand,' the show. It seems silly to me now. I thought I was making art, kind of."

"Maybe you were. Art has a life of its own. Even your own creation doesn't need your continued approval to be art."

"It certainly doesn't need my approval to play over and over on television. But it's not like I'm ashamed of it. I'm just done with it."

"I can see how that would be the case."

"No you can't. You're like a superhero. You cannot relate to me at all."

"I'll take your word for it." Ky laughed. "Am I allowed to admire you?"

"Maybe, I'll let you know." She smiled, and then her voice changed to concern. "What will happen to the senator and all those people who drank the blood?"

"Hopefully nothing." Ky's voice showed that he shared her concern.

"I took a sip. I spit it out."

Ky looked at her worried for a moment. "I think Henry would have tried to get you to do something if he could have controlled you; he wanted to finish me, so we would know. He could have sent you back upstairs. I suppose he could even have had you stab me."

"Yikes!"

"He knows I wouldn't…"

"Wouldn't what?"

"Fight back," Ky finished quickly. "But that is worrying. I'm glad you had the good sense to spit it out."

"I poured the rest of the glass on a plant and it died instantly. It was crazy. It was like a cartoon."

"Money isn't good for everything," Ky laughed. "Despite its almost universal appeal."

"It makes me wonder about my life," said Mimi. "Am I a bad person, just for being rich? Just for *liking* being rich? Is Dad? Actually, I'm not sure Dad likes being rich, but he is."

"At least he's not out for world domination."

"No; I may have been for a while, but not now. And now that I'm rich and very ill, now I'm really a mess. I'm like the person everybody wants to be and nobody wants to be at the same time." She kicked thoughtfully at tufts of grass.

"Do you want to be you?"

"I used to love being me. Then I hated it. Now I have mixed feelings about it, but mostly I'm afraid." She paused and then said, "I'm afraid to move forward."

Ky laughed. Mimi was surprised, but he said, "But you're not afraid of taking out a magical super-villain at the risk of your own life."

"I guess when the right thing to do smacks you in the face, you just kind of do it. Still, I hope Henry isn't secretly controlling me. That's really not, well, not what a girl wants, if you know what I'm saying."

"He can't control you from Or-ta. Plus I think if he were controlling you, you'd feel ill. When someone is controlling you like that, if they go away and don't give you direction, you feel as if all the color has been sucked out of the world."

"So the senator and his wife and all those party guests can resign themselves to being depressed for the rest of their lives?"

"Fortunately they had very little, but in essence, yes, they'll always feel as though something is missing. Once you are bound to someone, their absence creates a longing for which there is no contentment."

"I guess there are worse fates, like, if Henry had stayed around and they were his zombies. Ooooh, I really don't want to be a zombie!"

"Well, you don't look like a zombie; you look fine. You actually look like you have more of a healthy glow than I've seen you with yet."

"I guess I'm adjusting to my new normal. The limp, the pain, the seizures. They just are what they are. They're not everything I think about. Okay, they're still a lot of what I think about," she admitted. "But it's changing slowly. Maybe I'll be ready to make ditzy art again soon, who knows?"

"It's entirely up to you." He looked at her thoughtfully. "Mimi, I'm really grateful for what you did for me, me and all of humanity."

"You're welcome?" She looked away from him. Neither of them said it, but she knew it was time for him to leave. The park was thickly green, and yet still gave off a slight crackly, California dryness, as if it could catch fire any minute. The sky was a high, light, hazy blue. Standing there with Ky, she thought she'd never seen the park before, never seen anything before she met him. How would she live even a semi-normal life knowing that there was magic everywhere? She had partially lied about her new normal. Her new normal was Ky. She couldn't admit it to him, but she didn't know how she'd hold up once he flew away.

Ky spoke gently, almost as though he had read her mind. "Mimi, you can have those things that you want, the handsome husband, the kids. You don't have to do the show, but you can if you want to. Yes, you are very ill. But don't ever think you have nothing left to give."

She watched him walk toward a big oak tree, transform into a crow, fly up into the branches, look back at her, and then fly away. The strangest sensation came over her, as though she were flying with him and the world came into sharp focus. She thought she could see all the way down to the ocean and into the ocean, the fish in it, the sand falling away to the dark blue depths. She thought she could see up to the mountains where Ky circled around and was flying east. She could sense the weather, the cold, the wind at her back. There were colors she had never seen. She remembered back to the night when she picked him up from under Henry's library window, it was the same feeling. She was tempted to dive into the feeling, to follow Ky, but she shook her head to shake the feeling away. Colors returned to normal. The park was there, crackly, hazy, present. It was time for a new life, a whole new life. His words rang in her ears. *Don't ever think you have nothing left to give.*

Thank You

I'd like to thank my mother who very lovingly and enthusiastically edited all the books and stories I wrote in grade-school, and this one.

Kate and Laura Abbott, Jennifer Zurick, Mary-Kat Cone, Rebecca Wilson who has saved my life a thousand times, Brooke Parkhurst, Arthur Gillett, Terry Peterson, Lauren Peacock, Erin and Jon St. John, Lorran Garrison, Yvette Osborne, Heather Lukacs, Uncle Stuart, Walter Corbiere III, Michelle Treviño, Professor Thomas, Professor Menkhaus and Professor Hernandez-Chiroldes who wrote me the kindest words a student has ever read: "You are a writer."

Mrs. Kellogg, Coach Wallach, Fannie Chase, Terry Schreiber, Pat Souney—all those sweet sayings about teachers transforming your life, they are true.

For the most salient piece of advice ever given, I'd like to thank the late Greta Fertik.

Thanks Kylin Witte for being a legend.

For my continued good health I'd like to thank Dr. P, Julie Hwang, Peilee Ren, Robin Snyder, Ginger Danz, Rebecca Snow, Mariah Hibarger, Jim Maxwell, Ocean, Kate Lukacs, Jenny Becksted, Luke Hrabosky for the half days, Carlos Plumley for providing a cello in my darkest moment, Markus and my remarkable dog Pip.

And I'd like to thank my father for loving to travel with me. Pip wants to thank you for the delicious hotel breakfasts.